Reviews of *Sacred Objects*

- ❧ A memorable story about lasting friendship.
- ❧ A book that won't leave your mind for quite some time.
- ❧ A story of relationships, loyalty and kindness, knowing oneself, and following your dreams.
- ❧ The kind of book that makes you feel a range of emotions.
- ❧ Lovely, emotional, heartfelt.
- ❧ Written as a gently winding path through the forest, and the reader is being led along, with the occasional foray down a side track, but always coming back to the main path.
- ❧ It took me back to reading *Beloved* by Toni Morrison. Avery Kerr's style of writing is similar.

More Praise for *Sacred Objects*

Ms. Kerr writes of the personal desert of Laura, a bleak place, not of her own making, and of her discovery that often what seems like an oasis is only a mirage. With a deftness that compels belief, she traces Laura's quest for a life that will quench her thirst, the light she cannot see, but knows is there.

Christopher Britton, author of *Paybacks*

Sacred Objects is a compelling odyssey of discovery, a young woman's odyssey as she interacts with those who would abuse, and sometimes those who would lovingly guide. Avery Kerr's lyrical storytelling draws, then sweeps the reader into the experience.

Morris Crisci, author, *Golda, May You Someday Rest in Peace*

Sacred Objects, a coming of age tale, is the story of Laura McKenna. Early childhood memories of her raging father and submissive mother scar Laura's psyche. Her wounds lead to romantic heartbreak during her rebellious teenage years and emotionally crippling insecurity in relationships of every sort as a young adult. Peace for Laura, and command of her own destiny, will only come after she endures serial disappointments, tears and helpless fury.

Sound like something you've read before? It's not. This story is elevated above the ordinary by intricate, well-imagined words, carefully composed into lyrical passages that simply won't be found in many works of this genre.

H.G. Field, author of *Kickin' It*

や ら

Sacred Objects

By

Avery Kerr

Sacred Objects

Author: Avery Kerr

ISBN-13: 978-1533308047
ISBN-10: 1533308047

For permission, please contact:
Avery Kerr
avery.kerr@gmail.com

Bedtime Story by Lisel Mueller is reprinted with permission from Louisiana State University Press.

Cover design by Kari Cureton

Book layout/design by David Larson

Bedtime Story

The moon lies on the river
like a drop of oil.
The children come to the banks to be healed
of their wounds and bruises.
The fathers who gave them the wounds and bruises
come to be healed of their rage.

The mothers grow lovely; their faces soften,
the birds in their throats awake.
They all stand hand in hand
and the trees around them,
forever on the verge
of becoming one of them,
stop shuddering and speak their first word.

But that is not the beginning.
It is the end of the story,
and before we come to the end,
the mothers and fathers and children
must find their way to the river,
separately, with no one to guide them.
That is the long, pitiless part,
and it will scare you.

Lisel Mueller

The children are going to church even though it isn't
Sunday. On the way down the aisle, Gwen, five, presses
her hands over the skirt of her crisp, navy blue dress and sings
a song she made up. "Hush." Aunt Gladys has Margaret, three, by the hand and
carries their baby sister. Even at their young ages, both children
know hush is Southern for shut up.

Near the altar, a cross, swathed in black tulle, towers over
the coffin. Their aunt steers the children into the family pew.
The girls are not expected to view Mama's body, only to
remain quiet. Daddy stands to let the two children scoot down
the bench toward Mother's Mother. Once seated, Gwen
removes her small, cotton gloves. She stuffs one inside the
other and rolls the makeshift ball along the pew. Margaret
swings her legs back and forth, admiring her black patent
leather shoes.

Mother's Mother frowns. She has no patience for the
children, especially today. Near the turn of the century, her
forebears founded the church in Charlotte, but by now, 1926,
most family members had moved out of state. Only local
relatives and a few of Edith's university friends are present.
Mother's Mother wears her hair pinned back under a dark hat.
Not even a tendril can escape. Later she will reprimand Gladys
for dressing the girls in navy instead of black.

The pastor appears and a hymn begins, not one of the
triumphant anthems about the victory of eternal life over

death, but a dirge. The deep minor chords of the organ music wake the baby, but her cries can't be heard above the mournful melody. After the music, a Bible reading, and then a poem written by the deceased. Untraditional, but Mother's Mother wants to make sure everyone knows Edith was a college graduate, a woman of letters.

When she died of an overdose, the family attorney suggested a lawsuit, but the nurse on the maternity ward claims her patient hoarded the pain pills to take all at once. The hospital insists Edith suffered from postpartum depression. For propriety's sake, Mother's Mother decides to report the cause of death as pneumonia.

The service over, churchgoers step into a quintessential southern summer afternoon: emerald greens, cicadas humming, an almost wet sun. The children are driven to their grand-mother's home to wait for the mourners to arrive for a reception. At the house the little girls have their faces washed and hair brushed by Ivey, a thin, serious Negress, who's a bit rough. "Hush," she says when they protest.

The girls, told to play until the guests arrive, hide in the coat closet, a place they can count on not being used today. There's an overhead light, and they take a picture book and a doll they pretend to read to. The banquet table on the veranda holds a platter of flaky biscuits and ham. A colored man, holding a silver tray, offers glasses of lemonade and iced tea with fresh mint.

From inside the closet the girls hear the clinking of ice and Southern conversation. "We are all terribly grieved," a woman says to Mother's Mother.

"A tragedy, to be sure. Whatever will he do?" a man's voice asks. "He's got three young children, one of them a newborn." Margaret understands he is talking about Daddy.

"The older two are such bad little girls."

"We're bad," Gwen whispers.

Margaret starts to cry.

In less than a year, Daddy remarried, and Edith's girls inherited a step brother and sister. Whenever they misbehaved, the children knew Mama would not have been as stern as their other mother. In their minds Edith became an angel, a confidant, a curiosity, a woman to emulate.

On the way to womanhood, they compared themselves to Edith. Were they as smart, as pretty, as popular? They played a game of magical thinking well into their twenties. "If Mama was here, she'd bring white roses from her garden to the party. She'd write a special poem. She'd bring boxes of petit-fours that she proclaimed 'homemade' and everyone would laugh because we knew she couldn't bake." or "If Mama saw you in that dress, she'd have a conniption fit."

When Daddy's company transferred him to Cincinnati, and Mother's Mother found out her grandchildren would attend school with Negroes, she wrote, demanding he send them to her in Charlotte. Together she and Gladys would raise them as daughters of the South. He declined, and the family grew apart. No one up north knew about their dead mother, and the girls never mentioned her to their friends. It was a relief not to be identified with death.

Each of Edith's girls would marry a man named Bill. Among them they would have ten children. Becoming mothers made them long for her even more. Their imaginations shifted to deeper questions: had Edith been burdened by their care? Had she fought with Daddy? Even if she could have risen from the coffin at the foot of the cross, Edith could never have justified her actions. Her children would spend their lives unsatisfied. Everyone needed to believe her death was someone else's fault.

Edith, Gladys, Gwen, Frances, Mother's Mother, Ivey: the litany of names I grow up hearing. They are characters in a fairy tale that happened long ago in a distant land. My mom, Margaret, never tells the story the same way. Sometimes she says her older sister, Gwen, was forced to view their mother laid out at home. "A custom at the time," she explains. Although fascinated by my Southern heritage, I'm afraid of dead mothers, coffins, and closets.

We live in Louisville, close enough to visit the Cincinnati aunts, uncles, and cousins, but far enough away from North Carolina that visits are rare. Mom hated Cincinnati. "I have few good memories of that city. It was grey instead of green," she told us. No one in her junior high could understand her southern drawl, so she joined the Drama Club and left the melodic cadence of long a's and extra syllables behind. I make sure to enunciate clearly and do not want to leave my mother, ever.

On the first day of first grade I hug Mommy's knees and won't let go. My father pries my chubby fingers loose and carries me to the car. I'm wearing saddle shoes and a plaid skirt; my front tooth is loose. At the entrance of the huge building we're met by the principal who takes me from Dad and scoots me down the long dark hallway to a classroom. It's an old-fashioned school house, built in the twenties, with hardwood floors, lots of blackboards, and a musty smell. My little girl self can only imagine that monsters lurk in each dark corner. My stomach does flip flops. I feel as though I am leaving the world.

The teacher, Mrs. Sinkhorn, is mean and so old. She makes the class press really hard when we color. "And, children," she never calls us by our names, "you must outline everything with black." My fingers hurt.

The second morning I kick Dad and hyperventilate. That afternoon at school I throw up in the wastebasket. And so it goes on for what seems like forever. I cry-plead-beg not to have to go. My parents, deaf to hysterics, force me. All the dark, scary feelings, too big for a child's body and mind, blossom into a flower of amorphous dread.

Another dark fairy tale unfolds at home. My father has eaten my mother. She shifts from accommodating, to obedient, to servile. My sister, Meg, and I aren't allowed to eat dinner until "your father's had his drinks," at 7 or 8 in the evening, bedtime for most young children. Dinner's not about eating, but about blaming. Dad yells at either Mom or us kids, "I pay the bills around here." Justification not only for his unpleasant disposition, but also his escalating temper.

When we complain the least bit, he reminds us of our privileges. "Food, clothing, a roof over your heads. Not to mention braces, piano lessons. God-knows-what-else." He tells us he's worked since he was eleven, what great a country we live in, where a man can move up in the world. "Drugstore errand boy becomes regional manager." He has the right to say what goes on in his own home.

Dad told Mom when to go to bed, what to wear in public, and how he liked his bourbon mixed. Often he passed out on the family room couch, drunk, tranquilized, or both. Whiskey and pills guaranteed long dreamless naps. We'd turn up the TV so we could hear it over his snoring.

What would please him one day would cause him to fly into a rage the next. We'd enjoy a sandwich together, then he'd accuse me of making my fat face fatter. A pretty dress in the morning would make me look like a tramp after he had his first cocktail. Earning Dad's approval meant jumping through invisible hoops with no black outlines.

As a family, we seldom went out in public because Dad would create a scene. A tyrant at home, he carried an arsenal of commands and insults to restaurants, where undeserving servers bore the brunt of his disdain. A small detail, such as a wilted lettuce garnish or an unripe tomato slice, meant his meals went back to the kitchen. Meg and I ordered something simple and ate fast, so Dad couldn't find fault with our food as well.

In stores his flirtatious banter made female sales clerks uncomfortable; his angry rants tempted males to throw a punch. To be rid of him, most managers gave Dad his money back. In exchange, they asked him not to return.

We rarely went anywhere more than once, except church. By the time I turned twelve, I considered this adult hypocrisy. Although these upstanding, compassionate Christians must have suspected how bad life with Dad might be, no one came to our rescue. Just because a man kneels before the altar one morning a week does not make him a good man. That such a sinner could be welcomed in the house of God without retribution made me lose hope. Sunday services didn't stop

Dad from drinking. Beer for breakfast became beer for lunch. By noon he would be, in his own words, "half in the bag."

Each Christmas we'd go to the service the night before so he and Mom could have special breakfast drinks while we unwrapped presents. "A toast, ho-ho-ho, a toast to Christmas." Dad would hold up a Bloody Mary. "Where are my girls?" He'd pretend he couldn't see us. Meg and I were standing right in front of him. That's about as playful as he ever got.

By the time we reached middle school our mother was vague and dreamy. We used to think her Southern-ness lent her a kind of fragile beauty, but now we felt deserted. That's when she began to have difficulty driving. One afternoon after school, I found her dressed, but in bed. "Call a taxi, please, Laura." Her voice sounded tired. "We need to pick up your father at the airport. We'll eat dinner there and take the cab back home."

"Come on, Mom, we have a car—"

"I can't drive, Sugar." She rolled to one side. "Parking's so hard."

"But we go to the airport all the time." My father often travelled for work. Some weeks he'd be gone all five days, a blessing and respite. "It will be an adventure."

Mom sat up and hugged her knees. "Look up the number and call." She didn't sound right. "Please."

As soon as the taxi, a rare sight in suburbia, pulled into our driveway, a neighbor came across the street. "Everything all right, Margaret?" Mom gave the woman a wooden smile. Meg and I, embarrassed by the fuss, dove into the back seat. When the driver took Mom's arm and escorted her to the front, she looked at him as if he were a footman for Cinderella's coach. Dipping into the seat, she rolled down her window, and waved all the way down the street.

When she told Dad about the cab, the whole restaurant heard his response. "Picking me up is your job. The girls shouldn't ride with strangers." Mom stared at her plate. Meg grabbed my hand under the tablecloth. "Think I'm made of money?" he demanded.

Mom endured the public shaming in silence. At that point I understood two things: Dad was pissed off because she'd made her own decision, and we would have died if he'd gotten behind the wheel to drive us home. On the way home in the back of the cab, I felt protected by her ruse, but she would be punished for her treachery.

In the sixties, electroshock therapy promised an end to depression. The next morning Dad convinced a psychiatrist that Mom needed shock treatments. Our mother in the mental hospital, Meg and I fluctuated between embarrassment and fear. Dad told the neighbors she'd gone to Cincinnati for a family emergency. When he promised us she'd return soon, we didn't believe him. A woman came to clean and cook. Her greasy meals made me sick to my stomach.

During the month Mom was gone, Meg, in fifth grade, learned the facts of life from a film shown at school, but she had questions. When she tried Dad on the subject, his face reddened, and he handed her a book. The grainy, black and white enlarged photos of egg and sperm didn't help her understand sexual intercourse. Confused, she came to me. I'd seen the same film two years earlier, but couldn't explain the mechanics. I'd heard other kids using words I didn't want to share with my little sister. In addition, my developing body mystified me. I prayed my period wouldn't start during Mom's hospital stay. I couldn't ask Dad to buy pads, much less tell him I was bleeding. My womanhood, the only way out of the dark forest, needed to stay secret.

When Mom came home, she wasn't allowed to have visitors and slept the days away. My sister and I punished her for her absence. "Rip Van Stinkle," we called her, "Ratpunzel, Sleeping Cootie." A daytime nurse shook her awake every four hours to dole out medication.

Dad dismissed the cook. "You girls are old enough to make cereal and sandwiches. I'll get take-out for dinners."

After two weeks, Meg and I began to enjoy Zombie-Mom. Each afternoon we had a few hours to ourselves to watch TV and talk on the phone. By the time Dad arrived, burger bags or pizza box in hand, we'd always be in our rooms doing school work.

Within a few months, Mom resumed her household duties.

Several years later, when Dad put Mom in the hospital again, I visited her right after a shock treatment. Legs covered with a plaid blanket, she shrank back into an overstuffed chair. She looked smaller. "They made me take off my wedding ring." Throughout my childhood, Mom often sounded troubled and confused, but this fragile voice belonged to someone else. She picked up a paper cup and gulped water. "Where did you get that dress?"

"We bought it last spring," I said, when you came to see me at college."

"Oh." She glanced out the window at the rolling green hills. "Where do you go to college?"

I thought she must be joking, and gave her a half-smile. She repeated the question.

"Up in Indiana. Madison." My heart dropped into a vat of sadness. Intended to soften the memory of her mother's early death, the shock treatments created huge gaps in Mom's mental landscape. I don't know how much of my childhood she recalls, what I remember is distorted. All of us, victims of an evil spell.

At school, I became a model student, thriving on the praise of my teachers and mentors. My dedication to my studies increased. Mom's depression and Dad's alcoholism made me a fanciful child. Schoolwork done, I would read Oz or Narnia books, escaping into safer and more compelling worlds where the beasts had horns and hooves instead of highballs. At sixteen, after I saw *Dr. Zhivago*, I dropped the "u" from my given name. "Laura" was predictable; "Lara," exotic. It didn't stick.

Once I learned to drive, I visited the library daily. It was a refuge, an excuse to get out of the house. I didn't discuss my parents with anyone. How could I? What would I say? I invented practical strategies like going over to my friend Susie's house for dinner because her family ate at 5:30. That way the hole in my stomach wouldn't be from both stress and hunger. Susie lived within walking distance, and even if she wasn't home, I would go sit in her backyard. Mom and Dad were too tired or preoccupied to object when I came back just before dark.

"Laura. There you are." Mom acted almost surprised to see me, as if she forgot me each day until I appeared in the evening. "Please set the table."

"Sure, Mom." I pulled three silverware settings from the drawer and reached for the napkins. "I ate at Susie's."

"You'll join us just the same." Dad said.

"I've got homework."

Sometimes he would insist; others he'd let it go, and I'd retreat to the safety of my room. Often I felt guilty for leaving my sister alone at the dinner table, but I'd make it up to her later by singing her a special song at bedtime while brushing her hair.

I hate the smell of bourbon, especially Early Times Kentucky Straight Bourbon Whiskey. Several cases live in our basement. The golden color shines through clear half gallon bottles, as though something valuable were inside. Bourbon, the blood of the Englishman. The Giant, the one who swallowed my mother, drank bourbon.

Only twelve, I started to splash an ounce or two into film canisters or travel-size lotion bottles. My sister, girlfriends, and I would stroll down our dead-end street. We'd swing our legs over the concrete barrier, then climb the fence into a large field, land the developers hadn't gotten to yet. Susie would produce cigarettes, bent from riding in her pants pocket. We'd go through two matchbooks to get a light in the wind, only to be disappointed in the result. The smell and taste made us sick.

The sips of forbidden liquor made us heady. We took off our training bras and blouses to taunt the neighborhood boys who rode by on their bikes. We imagined our budding breasts would make them crawl with want, but the boys, content with cat-calls, hadn't reached the age of desire. Once, we got terrible sunburns across our chests. To avoid explanation, we sneaked Noxzema from the medicine cabinet. The twin appeal of risk and secrecy lured me into sin.

Booze made me a thief. After the kids I babysat went to sleep, I'd gather an inch or two of brandy or port from their parents' well-stocked bar. By the age of fifteen I'd tried enough kinds to develop a preference for liqueurs, sticky and sweet, daintily sipped, perfect and ladylike. Southern.

The first time I got drunk I looked right at Dad and said, "Good-night, Hank." At the time I was convinced my slip of the tongue caused his wrath. Never mind that my date, Hank, and I had passed out. Disregard the empty pint of Everclear, 190 proof. Forget the pair of chaperones who discovered us, looked at our licenses and drove us home.

I'd asked Hank, the super nice guy who sat behind me in homeroom, to the Sadie Hawkins Dance on a whim, and some seniors gave us the pint as a practical joke. I remember a long stumble through a hay field toward his car. Ever the gentleman, Hank reaches for the door handle, but I stagger into the tall grass and retch. Ever the young lady, I keep a hand over my mouth to stifle the noise. During my absence, my date settles into the back seat. I remember being pleased that he has blacked out first and can't smell my reek. Soon I join him in the same dark tunnel.

Voices. "Shall we call the police? Hand me her purse." By the time they ring the doorbell, I'm standing, and the world reels. My father steps out onto the front stoop and grabs my upper arm. While the adults explain the situation, he increases the pressure. A brief moment of lucid thinking advises me to go back outside and beg the chaperones to take me with them.

Dad marches me to bed. I topple onto the mattress. My world spins again. Eyes closed, or open, monsters everywhere. My father returns with a stack of folded towels, which he throws at my head. "Try not to drown in your own vomit."

The next day, knowing better than to offer an explanation, I accept my sentence in silence. "You're grounded. No Susie, no Saturday dance class." Dad, Orator, delivers the law. The veins on the side of his neck pulse. "No nothing." I smolder. How dare he punish me for getting drunk? To keep from boiling over, I stare at my hands and sing an Elvis song in my head. Dad picks up his suitcase and gives Mom a peck on the cheek. "Don't let Laura out." He makes me sound like the family dog.

I want to ask him how long the torture will last, but his smug iron-rule face discourages me. He'll be gone all week, on a road trip for business. I hope Mom will cave. I wish she'd answered the door the night of the dance. In my childhood game, like the one she played about her mother, she'd offer coffee, lie down in bed beside me, press a cold washcloth to my forehead.

Within three days, she let me come along to the grocery and to pick up Meg from school. I suspected this was her way of getting back at Dad. The afternoon before he returned, Mom took me clothes shopping. In the store we'd look at each other and say, "grounded" at the same time. We didn't giggle, but close.

My punishment lasted a month, and then life continued pretty much the way it had before the episode with Everclear. At school the seniors who pulled the prank bragged, but the hubbub soon died down. Hank's parents, the "boys will be boys" type, forgave their son's transgression. I was glad he didn't suffer. We didn't go out together again.

After the first round of shock treatments, one of Mom's last remnants of individuality revolved around her church participation. She brought religious tradition with her from the South. "Daddy," she might as well have said God, "my remaining parent, brought up his children in the Anglican Church. So will I." She drew her line and we toed it.

The altar, stained glass windows and dark wood pews offered a peaceful respite from the tension at home. The Book of Common Prayer was anything but common. The dense language of prayers for intricate rituals conjured images of mystery. Episcopalians celebrated Almighty God, the Creator, and Preserver. He was immortal, merciful, and glorious. We loved Him.

Jesus, too. When we were little, we both got a picture of Christ standing in the desert. Each Sunday we attended Church School we'd get a lily sticker to place under Jesus' feet. Meg and I had lilies over lilies, even lilies in the sky. We sang Bible songs over and over while we swayed, gaining momentum, on our backyard swing set. Our favorite: "I've got the peace that passeth understanding down in my heart, down in my heart, down in my heart to stay-ay-ay."

Mom explained that early Christians, both men and women, hid in caves and covered their heads, so bats wouldn't get tangled in their long hair. Episcopalian women wore hats. Young ladies wore chapel caps. When we were kids, Meg and I adored these lacey circlets. We collected special ones, delicate pink diamonds and longer flowing ovals that looked almost like veils.

"Not going to wear a doily on my head anymore, Mom," I announced one day. "Just not happening. Megs isn't either." I'd reached fifteen.

"Please don't be difficult, Laura. It's a sign of respect. You know better. And why you would drag your sister into it is beyond me."

"So much is beyond you, Mom."

"Laura, I understand you no longer think it's fashionable. But you must cover your head in church."

In the end we compromised with wide headbands. One of my mother's greatest talents was compromise. One of her greatest goals was keeping peace. Otherwise, the Giant might wake up and roar.

In addition to attending regular Sunday worship, Mom volunteered in the gift shop at the Episcopal Church Home. She joined the Daughters of the King, a group dedicated to prayer, religious education, and service. Eventually Meg and I went not only to services, but also to Church School and Teen Evangelists, where we couldn't keep up with the social dynamics. The kids wore better clothes and went to better schools. Their fathers weren't drunks.

"Saw you at A & W," Diana Woods whispered to me during Church School. She had big boobs; I did not. I disliked her for many reasons, but felt guilty, since I knew her from church and our mothers were friends. "Why can't you be more like Diana?" Mom would ask us. "She entered the Diocese's essay contest. Diana signed up for Bible Study." My sister and I wished Mom would stop talking about her. In reality she was a bore, a pest, and a spy. "You were with Susie." Super Snoop must have seen us pour the little bottle of rum into our cokes.

"Weren't you supposed to be at Bible Study?" I asked her. That's where I told my parents I was going.

"Oh, right." Diana gave me a little wink, as if we were friends, then pulled a compact from her purse and refreshed her lipstick.

In order to avoid my parents and other kids like Diana Woods, I joined a different church. I gave up the haughty Episcopalian ways, the elegant language of the Liturgy for the homier words of the Baptists. The Anglican sacrament known as "the outward and visible sign of an inward and spiritual grace," Holy Communion, became the Lord's Supper. Instead of a wafer on the tongue and wine from a chalice, I began eating bits of Saltines and drinking grape juice from tiny paper cups. Episcopalians dressed their babies in christening gowns and sprinkled Holy Water on them at the Baptismal Font. Baptists initiated adults by a near drowning of new members in public view. Fully conscious, draped in white, I gave myself to the waters of the Baptistry tank and left my family behind. Immersion would make me clean.

Pat, the Preacher's Kid, and his family, Southern Baptists, didn't drink, smoke, play cards, or dance. I'd seen him at school, but our paths seldom crossed. Up until church, we'd exchanged greetings in the hallways. In our teenage world popularity meant being ready to chug beer and do the Twist, and, for most, popularity was the sole purpose of attending school. Academic achievement, my claim to fame, earned faculty praise and a bit of peer admiration. I coasted on my reputation as a serious student. When I didn't show up at weekend parties, everyone assumed I was cracking the books. In reality, I hadn't been invited.

Despite his abstinence, Pat managed to break through all barriers. Elected Mr. Seneca High our senior year, he embodied remarkable qualities. His scores topped the SAT charts. Colleges courted him. Not only was he the president of the Junior Classical League, he also wrote for the school paper. He founded Young Missionaries and volunteered at the Kentucky Center for the Blind.

When I joined the church, Pat opened the door to his world and invited me in. Life with Pat flowed along in a steady stream of activities. We'd go to church in the morning, march for Civil Rights in the afternoon, have a study date in the evening.

As Pat and his Baptists took me away from home, Dad didn't notice. The choice to change churches hurt Mom, but she'd stopped exerting her opinions. Everything about my mother ended up being about my father. Since both parents deserted me, leaving me stranded in their hideous reality, I abandoned them back. All my heroes, Dorothy, Pollyanna, Peter Pan were orphans.

Dwight and Reba, a couple in their mid-thirties, adopted me. They held Youth Leadership Classes at the Baptist Church. Rather than relying solely on Scripture to impart religious instruction, Reba rewrote classic Bible stories into plays. Dwight directed; Pat and I starred. Our on-stage relationship blossomed. "Mother," Reba's Prodigal Son said, "Out there are women whose breasts shine like stars, but nothing compares to the glorious light of the Lord." When God created the world Reba-style, He wasn't sexist. All of her Bible women spoke up. Eve and Adam, not Adam and Eve, took joint responsibility for The Fall. Reba's version of Sarah and Abraham's story included a conversation about their sex life. Daring for Southern Baptists.

Whenever Pat and I visited Reba and Dwight's home, another new world opened. This couple gave me hope. Their disagreements were resolved with tenderness and humor, without yelling and blaming. Pat helped Dwight write a church newsletter; Reba and I cooked dinner together. My definition of family changed.

At school no one could fathom why Pat had chosen me over a cheerleader. Since we acted together at church, we won leading roles in the senior play. Again we played a couple, whose lines rippled with sexual innuendo. Before Pat, sex seemed maybe-someday. Now, I hoped to unlock its mysteries.

Pat wrote funny songs for me like "Laura, Laura, I adore ya" and ones with tender lyrics, too. "Laura, my dearest/you are the nearest/I can be/to ecstasy." He played variations of the chorus complete with guitar riffs. "That's so sweet," I would say. Despite the December cold, he serenaded me on my seventeenth birthday. Wearing a fake mustache and a red sash, he kneeled outside my bedroom window and sang *Besame Mucho. Kiss me, kiss me a lot*, in classical Spanish guitar style. Each word carried the steam of his breath.

Too busy for the kind of kissing that leads to sex, we held hands, hugged, gave back rubs. Pat, allergic to public displays of affection, wasn't exactly cold, merely lukewarm. Once, after we double dated with his sister and her beau, he told me he thought she had L.M.S.R.V.M., Low Moral Standards in the Rear View Mirror. Pretty sure the couple in the back seat had done nothing more than chastely kiss, I took this as a cue.

Desperate to please Pat, I watched my every step. Even though I was often spilling over with desire, I held back, waiting for him to want me. Once, on the way home after a church play, I removed my bra and stuffed it into my purse. When we hugged goodnight, I pressed my body into his and hoped.

"Oh my darling Laura." Pat spoke with a little catch in his breath. "Don't." He stepped back, putting me at arm's length. "Please."

"Pat. I want to." I ached for him. "Please."

When he walked to his car and drove away, I blamed the Baptists.

In my senior yearbook classmates drew stick figures holding hands and doodles of hearts with arrows through them. They wrote cute little verses: "When you are old, gray, all of that, don't despair, so is Pat" or "You & Patrick, how Fantastic!"

Yale, Columbia, and Harvard offered Pat scholarships in fields ranging from classical music to calculus. My acceptance letters came from the University of Kentucky and a small, liberal arts school in Indiana. Hanover College offered tuition assistance. Pat chose Yale; my family's finances forced me to Hanover.

Our separation came as a shock to both of us. Freshman year I stayed off limits to male students. The college published a "Wolf Book" in the summer so that eager older guys could see photos of the new co-eds who would arrive in September. Flattered, but firm, I turned down fifteen invitations for dates the first week of school. By January, everyone knew I was saving myself for Pat. Sorority sisters urged me to date anyway. "Come on, Laura. Keg party in the woods behind the Sigma Chi house."

I wasn't tempted. "Have fun. I'm going to study." My standard reply, one that had worked in high school.

"Charlie Yale coming down this weekend?"

During freshman year, Pat hitchhiked from Connecticut to Indiana at least a dozen times. Each day we talked on the phone. My earnings from babysitting jobs for children of faculty paid my long distance bills. During both winter and spring breaks we returned to Louisville, but Reba and Dwight had moved on to another church in Alabama. Without them, we had little social life.

Just before summer he proposed. Despite his long ride in the cab of a construction truck, Pat seemed energized. The spring night smelled of hyacinth and aster. We sat on a bench outside my dorm. When I rested my head on his shoulder, he took my hand. "Let's get married this summer."

Sitting up, I searched his eyes to see if he was serious. I couldn't tell. "Don't tease."

"Not teasing." Pat held my face between his hands. "I can't wait any longer." He pulled me closer. "Let's not miss our chance, sweetheart." He'd finally made the move.

In contrast to the way I had imagined the moment, our first real kiss felt silly, as if we were cartoon characters. Mickey and Minnie, Barney and Betty. To his credit, Pat didn't fumble, but his back remained rigid. Try as I might, I couldn't melt into him to become one being. Neither of us had much experience, but my body knew we would not make good lovers. My fantasies of sexual pleasure met a lack of passion. Unable to match his ardor, I broke the connection first.

"I don't have the ring yet." He wore the unfamiliar smile of a suitor. "Thought we'd choose together." He touched my finger where he planned to place a wedding band. His excitement made him oblivious to my lack of response. "Hate to disappoint, but you won't be a June bride. Reba and Dwight promised they'd come if we wait until August." As soon as he looked at my face, he stopped.

"I can't." My struggle for words slowed time. "We can't."

"Don't tease." He reached to bring me close again.

I pulled away before the kiss got started. "No."

"'No?' Just like that, 'no'? What have we been doing, then, Laura the last two years?"

"Being friends, best friends."

"We'll still be friends."

I stood. "We've never even made out, for God's sake." He cringed, most likely because I broke the Fourth Commandment, but I didn't care. Tired of being half of a goody-goody couple, I let my frustration, the hot lava of unrequited desire, come spewing out. "I thought you didn't want me." I gave him a minute to think about how that made me feel. "And now, all of a sudden, you show up, and everything's decided?" I didn't give him time to answer. "The schedule in your head has absolutely nothing to do with me."

"It has everything in the world to do with you." Pat got to his feet. Placing his hands on my shoulders, he turned me so that we were face to face, our bodies not touching. "Let me explain." I stepped back. He reached toward me. We looked as if we were doing a clumsy dance under the moonlight.

"Just go." I tapped his chest with both hands. He didn't argue. Courteous to the end, he turned away. "Please," I added, making sure he was far enough away not to hear me.

For the next half hour I waited outside, hoping he'd come back and start the night over. But when the air turned chilly, I climbed the steps to my third floor dorm room. Grateful that my roommate left campus for the weekend, I sobbed without restraint. The next day I waited by the phone at the end of the hall. At noon I walked to the boys' dorm where Pat bunked when he visited. No one had seen him. I went back to the phone. When Sunday became Monday, I forced myself to study for upcoming finals. Several times I considered calling him, but waves of sadness drowned out any words. A week passed, then another.

He sent a note:

> *Laura,*
>
> *Please forgive my advances and assumptions.*
> *Hope we can get together in Louisville.*
>
> *Fondly, Pat*

Somehow I got through the summer despite being under my parents' roof. We were past talking to each other about anything with depth or importance. Meg, like most children of broken parents, learned to be busy and absent. A job as camp counselor job kept her gone a month at a time. Salesclerk by day, waitress by night, I saved paychecks and tips toward my own getaway.

Pat called. We small-talked. Neither of us mentioned his proposal. Fearing friends would chide me, I avoided church and kept my mouth shut. In my mind a Greek chorus chanted: "You two are perfect together. Relax. Passion builds with time." Inside me a bubble of doubt formed, burst, billowed again.

In August, Diana Woods phoned on the pretense of planning a lunch for our moms, but actually to gloat. "Pat proposed to Sue." All the responses that rose to my lips would reveal my pain, and, when I didn't speak, she went on. "You know, the other gal in those church plays at Fairmont Baptist."

I knew. Sue, my understudy, the supporting actress in Reba's Bible plays, would make a suitable mate for Pat. Content to sew costumes or manage props, she wouldn't insist on sharing the spotlight. I pictured them ten years down the road: the ideal Christian couple, three apple-cheeked children, a two story house. Sex once a month.

The speed with which Pat had popped the question crushed me. As I relinquished my lead, the building blocks of my identity toppled. A crevasse opened. From the edge of a rocky cliff, I watched the rest of the world across a vast canyon. Nothing grabbed my attention. After Pat, disappointed by the anticlimax of our story, I guarded my heart.

Sophomore year I made up for every party I'd missed. I kissed any guy who showed interest. I got used to hearing "Come on, baby, you know you want to," used to saying "yes-yes, maybe, yes-yes, no." Debating the pros and cons of virginity, I earned my bad reputation and didn't care.

In spite of becoming a party girl I managed to maintain good grades. My academic standing bumped me up on the preferred housing list, allowing me to move from the dorm to Theta Annex. I shared this three-bedroom, white clapboard house with five other girls. Almost cozy, but I didn't bother to get to know my roommates and managed to avoid them. I'd had plenty of practice at home.

The campus, perched above the Ohio River, was surrounded by woods. The little house sat on the edge of a mid-western forest where gorgeous reds, oranges, and yellows signaled fall. One road, we called it "Devil's Backbone," zigzagged down to the water's edge. Previously paved, but never repaired or maintained, the road's asphalt buckled and cracked.

Weekday afternoons I got in the habit of drinking a beer or two, then wandering down the Backbone. I'd kick chunks of blacktop along in front of me. Sometimes one would roll off the road, and I'd listen for it to land at the bottom. In response to the sudden noise, a squirrel, rabbit, or an occasional grey fox might dart in and out of view. A roundtrip took almost three hours, and I'd squat to pee near the riverbank before heading back up the hill.

The sounds of the woods, birdcalls, rustling leaves, the scurry of small animals soothed me. When the leaves fell, I used my feet like whisk brooms to uncover the road. By mid-November the trees were bare, and around each curve I could see the road ahead. Near the river I looked around for a shrub that could offer privacy. Discovering none, I walked as close to the riverbank as I dared and hunkered down, exposing my rear end, trying to be quick because of the cold.

"Would you like to use my bathroom?" The voice came from behind me.

"Oh my God." Waddling until I could stand, I tugged at my jeans. My heart was pounding, but I didn't want to reveal my surprise and fear. One deep breath, standing tall, shoulders back, head high. "And where might your bathroom be?" I said, turning around.

Lovely. Dark, wavy hair, pulled back from her forehead by a bright pink headband, fell to her shoulders. Her bronze face wore a spray of light mocha freckles. She smiled, lovelier still. I relaxed.

"You've been here many times. Never noticed?" She pointed toward a narrow footpath that wound upward, opposite the direction I had traversed. "Follow me."

Curiosity won the fight with embarrassment and suspicion. I traipsed behind her. Since the house sat in a valley formed by gentle slopes, I could hear, but not see the river. The soothing echo of water, amplified one moment, diminished the next, reminded me of a washing machine. Mystery Woman opened the heavy wooden door. "Welcome. The bathroom's straight ahead on your left. I'll make tea." She nodded in the direction of the kitchen. "Come find me when you're through."

The house was as attractive as its occupant. Polished wood floors and wide doorways gave the indoors a spacious grace. Small, unexpected windows caught the afternoon light. The kitchen, maple cabinets and slate floor, all gleamed.

Pilialoha Katherine Moran Draper, Pia, turned out to be from California. In Indiana, 1968, she might as well have been from the moon. She was part Polynesian, which explained her honey skin and graceful sway. Her hands moved as she spoke;

her deep brown eyes narrowed and widened to emphasize the details of her story. She'd met Charley Draper, a truck driver, on the western leg of his route. After they married, he'd brought her east, at least as far as Indiana, where he deposited her with his kin while he drove. She told me all this as we waited for the kettle to boil.

"But newlyweds need privacy. Charley got this land cheap because it's too near the river. We built our house together." Pia reached into a high cupboard for two mugs. "It wasn't much to begin with." She looked up at the tinned ceiling. "We started with a simple frame." She paused. "Lots of scrap antique construction materials in these parts. He could build during long spells when the trucks weren't running." She turned her back to me while she poured. "When he got hurt, we had more time."

"Oh," was all I could think to say.

"He used a cane awhile, maybe six or seven years, before he had to go into a wheelchair." She took a breath. "Last year, around this time, Charley died." She faced forward again to hand me a mug of sweet smelling tea. "Doctors say cancer. I say his pride was hurt." She came closer and whispered, "You know, his manly pride." She poured tea for herself. "Come, sit." We moved to the living room. "His family gave us their furniture when they tired of it." She gestured at the worn velvet couch and mahogany coffee table. "Not my taste."

I sat in a puffy blue chair and looked at the photo displayed on the shelf next to me. The two of them, Charley and Pia, enraptured. She, in a halter top and shorts, flowers in her hair on Venice beach. He, tanned and muscular, wearing tight trunks, traces her bottom lip with his thumb to coax the smile. The photographer must have felt like a voyeur. "We didn't have kids." She cleared her throat. "A shame, really. My husband was quite the looker."

I agreed. They would have made beautiful children.

"Enough about me." She clapped once, softly, and then rubbed the palms of her hands together. "Your turn."

"Laura McKenna, born in Cincinnati. When I was three, my family moved to Kentucky." I wished for exotic ancestry and extraordinary events. "I go to Hanover College, just up the hill." I shrugged, unsure of what else to add. "I'll be nineteen next month."

My hostess nodded, waiting for more.

"Peeing in the woods is the most exciting thing I've done in my life so far."

That earned me another amazing smile. "Oh, I doubt that." She laughed. "I figured you were a college girl. I missed out."

"Not all it's cracked up to be," I said, thinking I might like to trade places with her, at least when her husband was alive.

"Charley had ten years on me." She leaned forward to look at the beach picture. "I worked at a truck stop diner the summer after I graduated from high school. Your age when we married."

Something moved me to speak. Maybe the late afternoon light, the whoosh-whoosh of the river, Pia's willingness to talk with a total stranger who'd been trespassing in her front yard for months. "My boyfriend proposed last spring."

She looked for a ring on my left hand. "Did you accept?"

"I couldn't." The moment my face froze in a half smile, Pia stood. I shrank back in my chair. As she came toward me I placed both hands in front of my chest to block contact. That didn't stop her. She gently separated my hands and bent to embrace me. Pia breached my personal canyon. From then on, no matter how I might struggle to climb back atop the cliff, I'd remember how she hugged me.

"But I'm okay." I choked, tears building in my throat. After a few moments, when my breath came evenly again, I reached for my jacket, thrown over the arm of the chair.

"Thanksgiving's next week." Pia backed up when I stood.

"Oh, right." I pulled a tissue from my pocket and wiped my eyes. "I forgot."

"Come for dinner? I'm a dynamite cook."

Surprised and flattered, I couldn't imagine she was serious. Even as my refusal formed, I thought about how wonderful it would be to miss the holiday at home. "Thanks, I'd love to, but school closes down. No students allowed in college housing over the break."

"Then spend the long weekend here. We'll eat and tell stories." Her smooth, animated face made her look younger than me. "Slumber party." Shaping her hands into talking mouths, she laughed. If she'd had children, they would have been gorgeous, as well as blessed. One afternoon, and I wanted her as family. "Okay." I paused, my voice still full of tears. "Wednesday after class? Five-ish?"

She nodded as we headed toward the door.

"I'll need to stay until Sunday, late morning."

We walked out front. "Not a problem," she said.

Thinking about carrying grocery sacks down two miles of switchbacks, I looked for a driveway. "How do most people get here?"

"Highway 97." Pia pointed backward. "Past the exit for the college is a slight left turn, Raven's Ridge. Hidden dirt road, about a half mile long, curves around behind the house." She walked me down two steps. "Don't get many drop-ins." She smiled. "Planned it that way."

For a moment I fantasized about what it would be like to live in the woods, undisturbed, with a husband like hers.

"Need a ride?" Her practical question interrupted my romantic reverie.

"I can get one with a sorority sister."

"Ask her to drop you off up near the highway. It's an easy walk."

"What would you like me to bring?" The annex had a small kitchen. "Maybe I could bake a pumpkin pie."

"Only your overnight bag," she said. "I'll get the food. We'll cook together."

I told my parents I planned to spend the holiday with a girl from Indianapolis. I told the girl from Indianapolis that if my folks called to tell them I was out walking. My sister, thanks to an Italian language scholarship, would be in Rome, where the holiday wouldn't be celebrated. My parents, involved in their own drunken banquet, wouldn't call anyway. Not a single person except me, and my hostess, would know where I was for three whole days. I was heady with power.

Pia planned our Thanksgiving Hawaiian style, with steamed mahi-mahi, pineapple cranberries, and coconut pie. We strung together leis made of pine cones and berries. "Ever had a mai-tai?" she asked.

"I don't think so." Of course I had not.

"Believe me, you'd know."

"The trick's not to use any juice. Light rum, dark rum, orange curacao." She pulled the bottles from the liquor cabinet one by one, each accompanied by a dramatic flick of her wrist and wiggle of her hips. She went to the fridge. "Fresh lime." She held it up, soliciting my admiration. "Orgeat syrup. It's almond, smell." Pia held the bottle under my nose. "And icky-sticky maraschino cherries." She put one in my mouth and handed me a full glass.

After a sip I couldn't talk for nearly a minute. "Wow."

"Surely it's better than that."

"Potent." The syrupy sweetness slid across my tongue, and then the rum hit my belly like a low burning furnace.

"I say if you're going to drink, go exotic and tropical. *"Á Kålè ma' luna,* Hawaiian for 'cheers.'" Pia held up her glass and we clinked. Unable to capture her lyrical expression, I parroted the words.

"Let's have some music," Pia said. The small stereo record player sat on a table in the hallway near the living room. "Turn up the volume so we can sing along in the kitchen. Pick out something you like."

My musical tastes leaned in the same direction as the popular culture: Beatles, Beach Boys, Credence, Rolling Stones. Listening to Otis Redding or Marvin Gaye made me feel righteously liberal. I flipped through her records: Elvis, Sinatra, Ella Fitzgerald. Turns out Pia didn't own a single album released after 1955. "How about Nat King Cole?" "Okay," she called from the kitchen. "Play the one with the couple on the cover, 'For Love,' or something like that." We swayed and sashayed to "Autumn Leaves." With Pia everything was a dance. The spectacular drink lasted through our late afternoon dinner. She didn't offer another. Before we ate, Pia took both my hands in hers. "*Mahalo* for this day, this food, this friend," she prayed. "Amen," we said together.

Our dinner conversation wove in and out, as we shared memories of Thanksgivings past, hers far more interesting than mine. "My mother's half Polynesian. We never celebrated like the pilgrims." Pia stopped to take a bite. "When I was a kid, we lived in San Ramon, rural enough that we built a pit, an *imu*, out back. We'd roast a whole pig, *kālua* style and invite the neighbors."

Trying to imagine such a scene on my street, I smiled in amazement.

"Hawaii wasn't a state yet. Tutu, my grandma, visited us for a month or two at a time. She taught me how to cook and dance." Pia swirled her fork through the cranberries. "And pray."

"My Dad's mom and her sister ran a candy store." I tried to think of something interesting to add. "They were puffy, perfumed old ladies who believed in giving children sweets and money. Along with pumpkin pie we ate chocolates and caramels." I didn't tell her about Edith, my maternal grandmother, who had killed herself when Mom was only five. I always wondered what she might have taught me. The sentiment must have made me look sad, because Pia started to tell funny stories about her cousins in an effort to cheer me. "Nakoa, Nicky, is like my little brother. We grew up together." She shook her head. "Well, one of us grew up, anyway."

"How old is he?"

"Twenty-nine? Thirty? I lose track. Younger than me by a few years."

"And you are?" I took this chance to ask my burning question.

"Thirty-five, soon. Seemed ancient when I was your age. Adult, but not old. Right?" She asked, flashing her beautiful smile.

I had to agree. The thirty-five year olds I knew, the moms of kids I used to babysit, wore bright red lipstick and went to the beauty parlor every week. They played bridge, hired maids to do the housework, and cared about what other people thought. Pia clearly did not. Her natural beauty, heightened by her isolated lifestyle, surpassed their efforts. "You don't look your age at all."

"Believe it or not, I wasn't fishing for a compliment." She stood to clear some plates.

"And," I said, "I'm being honest."

After we ate, Pia made Kona coffee, another rarity for me in a day of firsts. "Where do you get all this stuff?" I asked while we cleaned up. "Like the coffee and the coconut, even the fish. Madison Market sure doesn't carry it. I don't know any place in Louisville that would either."

"From Nick, the cousin I told you about. He still lives up near San Francisco. Comes through each month. Always makes sure I'm well stocked."

She pointed toward a small closet off the kitchen that served as a pantry. The entry was narrow. No door or light switch. I poked my head inside. Jars and tins lined the shelves that reached from floor to ceiling. "Do me a favor, please?" Pia dragged out a two-step folding ladder from behind the kitchen door. "See if there are any brown sugar cubes lurking behind the palm hearts, would you? The box with a picture of a parrot."

"Sure." I noticed the colorful labels. Most foods I'd never seen before. "Looks like a specialty store."

As Pia headed back to the dining room, I climbed up, stood on tiptoe, pushed the canned palm hearts aside, saw the box with the parrot. The shelves were deep. Six or seven cans of various foods tumbled down. Hearing the clatter, Pia came running. By the time she stood in the door frame of the closet, I was backing down carefully, the sugar box in the crook of my arm. Reaching the floor, I bent to retrieve the fallen cans. "Sorry. No broken jars, at least."

"Leave them," Pia instructed. "For later. Obviously I need to reorganize."

"Let me help." I started to pick up the cans.

"No." She made a quick reach into the food cupboard and pulled me out. "It's embarrassing."

Setting the box of sugar cubes down on the counter, I tried to go back into the pantry, but her hand stayed around my wrist. "Pour yourself another cup of Kona." Releasing her grip, she shooed me toward the coffee maker, then clenched both hands at her sides, impatient to attack the mess.

I took my coffee out onto the front porch. No doubt Pia wished me out of her way. Puzzled, I wandered down to the river and watched the grey clouds gather to cover the sun. As I climbed back up to the house, the porch light blinked on, guiding me through the trees. Peering through the curtain-less window, I watched Pia talk on the phone. Both hands gripped the receiver. She paced as far as the cord would allow, turning in a stationary circle, tangled until she needed to unwind. I couldn't hear the conversation, but noticed she spoke in staccato bursts. As soon as my hand touched the knob she hung up.

"Have a good walk?" The sudden question, meant to divert my attention from the phone call, didn't require an answer. "Thought we might spend the evening reading." Pia went to a large bookshelf. "I read poetry aloud to Charley, especially at the end." Her hands searched through a pile of paperbacks.

"Wait." I extracted a massive tome from my bag.

"Oh, beautiful. Let me see." Pia reached out. Taking the volume from me with both hands, she plopped into a chair, as if its sheer weight pushed her down. She ran her hands over the cover and binding, then turned to the title page.

Pleased that she seemed impressed, I savored the moment before breaking the spell. "It's nothing special, though. Not a first edition."

"Shakespeare was always special in our house." Pia continued to caress the large volume. "My father named me Katherine after one of his favorite characters."

"Kate, from *Taming of the Shrew.*"

"Smart girl."

"Yes, she was." I agreed.

"I meant you." Pia looked at me with admiration, as if I were some kind of quiz kid who'd gotten the answer right.

"Oh. Okay. Thanks."

"Dad went off on a business trip when I was a month old. When my grandmother from Hawaii came to visit, she christened me in her own style. I've been Pilialoha, Pia, ever since."

"So you were never called *Kate?*"

"My father's private name for me. He made me memorize this passage when I was ten." Pia stood and handed the book to me. "Read along. Act Two, Scene One."

Finding the excerpt took a bit of time, and Pia practiced breathing from her diaphragm. I could picture the freckle faced ten-year-old, wishing to please her father. She pivoted, right side toward me, and drew herself up proudly to speak to an invisible suitor:

Katherina: Well you have heard, but something hard of hearing
They call me Katherine that do talk of me.

Then Pia turned so that I could see her left side to respond:

Petruchio: You lie, in faith, for you are call'd plain Kate,
And bonny Kate, and sometimes Kate the curst;
But Kate, the prettiest Kate in Christendom,
        Kate of Kate Hall—

The recitation stopped abruptly. "Come on, I want to show you something."

Pia pulled me from my chair. She grabbed a flashlight from a table near the back door and led me out into the chill. Immediately I shivered and wrapped my arms around my shoulders. Both the little rum furnace and the warmth of the hot sweet coffee burned off.

"Don't worry, this will be quick. I won't let you freeze." We crossed the yard to a small garden. We hurried through a few pumpkins and winter squash until she kicked away some woody root stems. Her light shone on a large standing stone. At first I thought it served as a grave marker for a pet, then I worried her husband might be buried there. Someone had taken great care to etch the rock. Leaves of all seasons: dogwood, maple, oak, ash, were chiseled around the border. Two words in elegant script filled the center: Kate Hall. "Charley carved this after he got hurt. He had strong arms."

The stone captured my entire being. Without the vocabulary to express appreciation of such art, dedication, or sentiment, I stood in reverent silence. I couldn't imagine being loved so much by anyone. "It's beautiful. Amazing."

"Yes, it is. He was." She lifted the flashlight, aiming the beam toward a small white cottage. "And he chose the perfect name for my studio." Three small steps led up to an arched doorway. "My sanctuary, your bedroom." Pia stepped back to let me go in first. "No heat, but two down comforters on the bed should keep you toasty." She flipped the light switch. The painted murals created a brilliant floral paradise. A pair of palm trees framed the head of the bed, plumeria bushes bloomed along the floorboards. Sunlight, captured on the walls, radiated throughout the room. I stopped shivering and inhaled, expecting to breathe in the scent of jasmine.

"I'll be fine," I said, sure the colors alone would keep me warm. "You're both amazing." I turned in a slow circle, noticing details: two mynas in a flowering tree, a tiny crested cardinal hopping along a shell-covered trail.

"This kept me sane while Charley withered. One mural's still not finished."

"It's perfect."

"It's not entirely realistic." She sounded proud and apologetic at the same time. "I painted from childhood memories, enhanced by imagination."

"Childhood in paradise, that's for sure." My wonder grew each time I discovered another flower or bird.

"I create here. The place cheers me, especially in winter." She walked over to and opened the doors of a tall maple cupboard to reveal shelves, some piled with skeins of yarn, others with jars of beads. She pulled out the large bottom drawer and showed me pens, colored pencils, sketch books of all sizes.

We hurried back through the yard, heading for the warmth of the living room. "I've kept some of Charley's favorite clothes; his shaving cream's still in the medicine cabinet." She looked at my face for a reaction. "Sentimental, I know, maybe even maudlin, but I'm not ready to let go."

We sat in silence for a moment.

"Sometimes I have to talk about him to keep him alive, in here." She touched her heart and glanced at their beach photograph. "1954. Back then, good girls didn't flirt or make out. Any public display of affection was frowned upon. If you wore too much make up, showed your legs, or petted, you'd be labeled 'loose.' Once that happened, you'd have no friends."

"Nothing's really changed." I thought of my own growing reputation.

"That's too bad." Pia shook her head. "Dad paid my tuition to an all girls' school, and I didn't have much experience with boys."

"Lucky."

"You sound jaded." Pia examined my face. "Especially for your age."

"Confused, mostly."

She nodded, then continued her story. "The argument with my father started when I wanted my own money to spend as I pleased—"

"And a chance to get out of the house." I identified so far.

"Within a week, I managed to get myself a job waitressing. One morning, Dad caught me leaving the house for lunch shift. I wore a blouse that stretched tightly across my chest and bared my midriff." Pia pulled up her blouse to demonstrate.

"For bottoms, we wore red-checked pedal pushers that left no curve to the imagination. Dad hit the roof." Pia spread her arms wide. "Actually more like the outer stratosphere."

"My closet's got its share of Dad-angering outfits."

"'Miss Kate,'" Pia lowered her voice and bellowed, "'you are not going out in public dressed like a tramp.'"

"'Dad, it's my uniform,' I protested. 'All the girls wear them.'"

"'You are not all girls, you are my girl.'" She pointed her finger sternly. "Then he commanded me to stay behind the counter."

"I obeyed for about a month. Until Charley walked in. Tattoos, bulging biceps, gorgeous blue eyes."

"I'm guessing he didn't look like your average trucker."

"One of the other girls saw him coming and called, 'Hey, ladies, Spec-i-man, comin' through the front door.' I wiped down the counter, stared him right in the face. He moved toward a stool and said, 'What's for lunch?' in a kind of hillbilly accent."

"Did you say something clever?"

"No. Too busy swooning. Besides, all eyes were upon us. Knowing enough to act quickly before one of the other girls came to take his order, I handed him a giant soda and a burger that was waiting for another customer."

"Good move."

"Charley would always claim he got hit by the proverbial thunderbolt, but I remember he looked around plenty, before and after he made it up to the counter, so to speak." She looked down at her hands and twirled her wedding ring around. "I'm pretty sure he never cheated on me. Not certain, though. He kept driving full time for nearly five years after we got married. And he was so breathtakingly good looking that women paid him a lot of attention. So I wouldn't be surprised, or even particularly upset if he strayed."

Stunned, I couldn't find any words to respond. Episcopalians and Baptists had rules about adultery. Why would a guy with a wife like Pia ever look at another woman? Maybe my man would cheat on me some day. How unbearably sad.

"What's the matter?" Pia asked, sensitive to my swell of emotion.

I took a breath. "I don't know,"

"Laura, come on, tell me what's bothering you."

"I wanted sex with Pat for so long." My voice wavered. "I saved myself for him. And now he's engaged to someone else."

"You're jealous?"

"No, not really."

Pia raised her eyebrows.

"Marriage means being faithful, right? Otherwise, what's the point?"

"Sounds to me like your moral universe is pretty fragile." Her scrutiny made me shift in my chair. Pia stood, took one of my hands and helped me up. "And that you're ready for bed. Bring your backpack."

The cold air in the studio forced me under the quilts. A nightlight spread shadows across the walls. Tonight I would sleep in an enchanted forest. Before she left me, Pia kissed my forehead, Glinda protecting Dorothy. As a child, I had fantasized that my real family would come for me some day.

Pia could be my young aunt, an undiscovered cousin, an older sister. Most importantly, she could be my secret.

When the real sun streamed into the studio, touching the rays of the painted one, I awoke. Thinking Pia would expect me, I didn't knock. Again, as soon as she sensed my presence, she hung up the phone. "Sorry."

"What for?" No mention of the call, change of subject. "Breakfast?" While she placed a bowl and spoon in front of me, I sat at the table, a little girl on a school day morning. She served oatmeal with butter and brown sugar. "Thought we'd walk up to the reservoir today." Pia stood at the counter and chopped celery into turkey salad. "Maybe take a picnic?"

"Okay, let me help."

"Finish your cereal first."

"Yes, ma'am." I wanted to say "Mom," but thought she might take offense about her age.

"Oops, my bossiness must be showing." She sliced bread from a wide loaf. "Charley always told me I'd make a great school teacher."

"My parents want me to teach." I said between mouthfuls.

"But you have a different major in mind." Pia sealed the sandwiches with Saran Wrap.

I nodded, but let the conversation end there. I took the last bite and brought my bowl over to the sink. Following her instructions, I filled two thermoses with coffee. Pia selected hats, gloves, and scarves from a basket near the door. "We won't need these by noon," she said as we bundled up, "probably be sorry." She tucked her hair under a colorful knit cap. "But right now I can see my breath inside." She exhaled to make her point.

The phone rang. Pia ignored the noise and pushed me forward, closing the door behind us. "I told him not to call back until Sunday." Her hands made fists.

I wanted to ask questions: Him, who? What did he want? Why did she get upset each time he called? But I decided to wait and see if she confided in me. Then maybe I'd get a chance to earn her trust.

We hiked. Since there was no clear trail, Pia went first. Following, I wished for her grace, ease, and beauty. At first she picked up every rock in our path, said "thank you," and set it down off to one side. Looking back, I saw she'd created a trail. Gently pushing away low branches with gloved hands, she said "*E kala mai iá ú*, excuse me." Once or twice she turned around to make sure I was still behind her. "My grandmother," she called over her shoulder, "taught me to respect every living thing. Tutu told me rocks are alive."

Two hours later Pia and I climbed the sloping concrete face of one of the smaller dams. At the top we looked across the narrow, muddy Ohio. The river wound through the geography of my life, and I'd rarely seen it look beautiful. Just as predicted, our warm clothes were no longer necessary. We folded our scarves into cushions to sit on while we ate. "The water's much prettier near Evansville." Pia pointed. "South, then west, maybe a hundred fifty miles." My eyes followed that direction. "Ever hear of Angel Mounds?"

"I don't think so," I replied, intrigued by the name.

"Near the Draper family farm where we used to live. Let's go in April."

"I'd like to." My heart sped up with the idea that Pia planned on knowing me that long.

"Beautiful farm country. Lush green river bank. Trees bloom all spring. Charley would bring me armfuls of forsythia and crabapple branches. I'd hammer down the stems and put them in jars all over the farm house." We both inhaled, as if to conjure the scent. Everything she told me about life with her husband made me envious. My college education paled against her knowledge of what it meant to be loved.

When we returned from our hike, my feet ached. I rinsed the thermoses, restored scarves and gloves to the basket, and sat in the living room. After Pia lit the wood stove she went to the kitchen. I could hear her in the pantry. A few minutes later she came out with two full grocery bags. "I need to take this stuff over to the church before six. They're having a seasonal food drive." As she headed for the front door, I tried to catch a glimpse of what was in the bags, but she moved with quick steps, tense again. "Make dinner for us? I expect to be back in an hour or so." She grabbed her purse.

"All right." My stomach twisted into a knot.

"There should be lots of leftovers from yesterday."

Right after Pia left, full-blown anxiety arrived. My mother didn't cook well. Her predictable meals: meat, starch, salad, ice-box cookies, failed to impress. The southern kitchen of her childhood had been run by black women who produced excellent food and kept their recipes secret. Determined to please my hostess, I boiled pasta noodles and reheated the mahi-mahi. Adding eggs, cream, and sugar to the pineapple cranberry made a sweet pudding. I felt adventurous. The cupboards revealed lovely white china. In the pantry I found canned asparagus and a jar of sweet red peppers for color.

Pia returned in a cloud of noise. I heard the door slam, the scrape of her boots on the bristly mat, the wood stove being reloaded. "Still in the kitchen," I called. "Everything's ready." I lit candles and dimmed the light switch.

As she stared at the table without speaking, I wondered if I had done something wrong, like use her special wedding dishes. Maybe no one but she and her husband had ever eaten off these plates. An apology rose to my lips, but she spoke first. "Candles." She sat down and motioned for me to join her. She ran her finger around the rim of her plate. Again I feared a blunder.

"Aren't you going to eat?" I asked.

Pia unfolded her napkin with a flourish. "Good manners require me to wait."

I picked up my fork and she did the same. "I thought the hostess gave the cue to start."

"In my house the cook gets respect."

"I like your rules."

"Only some of them." Before I could respond, she tasted the pasta dish. "Mmm, good girl. Not too mushy or sweet."

I relished her praise. "Whenever I'd offered to cook for my family, my mother would say. 'Oh, no thanks, Laura, honey. We'll call for pizza. You can go pick it up.' Mom thought of fetching take-out meals as a reward."

She laughed. "You're well on your way to becoming a fine cook."

"Thank you."

"Thank you. No one's done anything as nice as this," she gestured to the candlesticks and place settings, "for me in a very long time." Pia leaned back in her chair, shoulders soft, face relaxed.

That night, I carried my pride at having pleased her to bed with me.

On Saturday I helped gather kindling, which took most of the day because Pia kept talking to each little twig. "What are you saying?" I asked. "Do they talk back?"

"First I thank them, then explain we use them for *ahi*, fire. I tell them we work in harmony, *lokahi*. Tutu would be able to hear their answers, but I can't." She cradled an armful of dry branches.

"You're a pioneer woman," I said.

"Hardly. Charley would have preferred a more rustic existence, like no indoor plumbing. He'd have been happy reading by candlelight, but I like my creature comforts. After his accident he couldn't gather firewood any more. Now his brother delivers a cord or two. I can manage chopping it into smaller chunks."

"Show me how. I'll help."

I learned about hard woods and soft woods, about which woods burn best for a quick, hot fire, and which woods you want to load before bed to give off a slow, steady burn. Oak would last all night. Throw pine on the embers in the morning. An axe requires two hands, a hatchet one.

"Thank Benjamin Franklin for the cast iron stove. It's far more efficient for heating than the fireplace," she told me as we loaded the wood bin.

Later we sat by the fire and snapped necklaces together. Tubs of colorful plastic beads, brought from the studio supply cabinet, sat on the coffee table. "Poppers," I said. "I haven't seen them since Saint Paul's Summer Camp."

Pia held up a completed strand. "These go to kids in the hospital. At first I thought only the girls would like them, but turns out the boys enjoy giving them to their little sweethearts."

My creations took me twice as long and weren't as attractive as hers. When I held up a string of alternating turquoise and bright yellow, my hostess nodded her approval. The sounds of the crackling fire blended with the occasional tiny explosion made when I made a mistake and had to pull one bead from another. Pia finished five necklaces and laid them across the table. She stretched and yawned.

"Go on." My eyes moved in the direction of her bedroom. "I can put myself to bed after I finish a couple more."

"Church camp?"

I was busy lining up beads, trying to come up with a new color pattern. "What?"

"Are you religious?"

"Yeah," I said. "I mean, I guess so. My mom's big on the Episcopal church. Pat and I met at First Baptist." I kept talking while I popped a purple bead onto a row of neon green. "He's the pastor's son."

"Do you believe in evil?"

The question stopped me. I put down the necklace. "Most people want to know if I believe in God."

"I'm not most people." Pia smiled, knowing I'd recognize her father's words.

"So I've noticed." Our repartee lightened the mood. "What do you mean by 'evil?'" I picked up the strand and searched for another bead.

Pia stretched again. She rose from her chair, came over to mine. "Too late to talk anymore." She bent to give me a brief hug. "Sleep tight."

Tucked under the quilts, I lay awake, pondering her question. The wicked characters in my beloved books seemed bad in contrast to characters who personified good. But evil? Dad's nasty moods carried bushels of unkindness. Alcohol made him mean. But evil? Church doctrine equated evil with sin. About this issue I remained undecided. In response to Pia, more important questions came. Why was she asking? And why me?

Sunday morning, I suggested we read from Shakespeare. I chose scenes from third acts, since I'd recently learned that's where the climax is. "Let's concentrate on the tragedies," I said. "They're more powerful." I was showing off, and Pia knew it. She let me get away with my college kid sense of superiority anyway. We spent half an hour going back and forth between *Hamlet* and *Othello*. I pegged her for Gertrude or Desdemona, but, insisting she was no tragic heroine, she left those parts to me. Instead she read the villains, Claudius and Iago. I wondered if her choice had anything to do with her inquiry from the night before, but dropped the subject.

Around eleven, I gathered my clothes. "I've got an afternoon study session back at school." I said "thank you" six or seven times. "See ya," I called back over my shoulder as Pia waved goodbye from the doorway. I worried, nervous about how and when that might happen. Did she assume I would continue my treks down Devil's Backbone? Would she watch for me? Carrying my backpack up the road to the highway, I stuck out my thumb. Ten minutes later I was crammed into a car of coeds heading back to campus. I felt as though I'd been away, in another country, for years.

The first two weeks of December brought snow, along with finals. I couldn't have walked to Pia's house, even though I wanted to. Finishing tests and papers left me no time to become distraught, only mildly obsessed. Campus would be shut down entirely for three weeks, no chance to see her until January. An eternity.

Even then I would have no address or phone number. I'd bought her a gift, a slim volume of Shakespeare's Sonnets. "Be patient," I told myself. "It doesn't have to be a Christmas gift." I didn't know Pia Draper well enough to know if she celebrated Christmas. Perhaps she honored a sacred traditional Hawaiian winter holiday. Maybe another college student would be joining her at the little house in the woods.

My last exam was at 9 am and my ride to Louisville wasn't leaving until noon, so I stopped by the Campus Center to check for mail one last time. Pia stood directly in front the wall of mailboxes. "Hi!" I put my pack down on a bench and gave her a tight hug. "Hi, hi, hi."

"Thanks for being so glad to see me," she said after I let go.

"Wait. I got you something. It's not with me, though." I sounded apologetic, as if I should have been prepared to see her. "Do you have a minute?"

"Sure." She handed me a box. "Promise not to open this until Christmas Day. Please."

I raised my hand as if taking a courtroom oath. "I, Laura McKenna, solemnly swear." That earned me one of her glorious smiles. "Now, come with me." I wanted to link arms, or lead her by the hand, but worried she would think me immature. Instead I walked right beside her, using my shoulder to guide us.

We strolled across the Quad, then walked by the nearly empty dorms and Greek houses. Right before we reached the Theta Annex a professionally dressed woman, whom I recognized as a biology teacher, walked up to us. "Pia?"

Pia blushed, not the usual bright red flush of fair-skinned folk, but a deeper scarlet hue that gave her honey skin a beautiful glow. When Pia leaned toward me and held my upper arm, I noticed her hurried breath. Using me as a shield, she managed to hide her discomfort from the other woman. "Hello, Janet."

Janet looked at Pia while extending her hand to me. "Hello. Janet Draper Lowell, biology professor. And you are?"

"Friend of mine," Pia said in a hurry.

Janet wasn't the slightest bit interested in me. She scrutinized Pia. "You've changed." It sounded like an accusation.

Pia took her time to find the response. "We all have."

"After you finished the house, we barely saw you at the farm. By the time Charley died, it had been what ... two, three years?"

"Once he was in the wheelchair, he just didn't want—"

"To see his family?" Janet shook her head. "I'll never believe that. He loved us."

"Of course he loved you all. But everything changed." Pia tightened her grip on my arm.

"First the wreck, then the cancer. He lived in constant pain."

An interloper in a conversation that should have been private, I looked at my feet. Neither of them seemed to mind my presence, and Janet continued. "Well, Mama and Pop felt deserted. Maybe you could explain all your reasons to them some time." She checked her jeweled wristwatch. "I've got a final to give, then we're off to Indianapolis. Spending holidays with Jim's folks. I'll call you when the rest of the family comes back up from Florida."

"I look forward to it," Pia said without a trace of sarcasm in her voice, merely a hint of resignation. But even I, who barely knew her, could tell she definitely wasn't looking forward to speaking with this woman again.

"Take care, then." Janet headed for the biology lab.

"I'm sorry you had to hear that," Pia said quietly.

"My family's no picnic." We reached my room, and I sat on my twin bed, motioning for her to join me. The house was empty, and that meant no introductions, interruptions, or forced holiday greetings. "And it sounds like you'll work things out soon." I kicked myself for sounding like Ann Landers.

Pia didn't seem to take offense. "Janet's hostility is nothing new. The Draper family has resented me since Charley drove up to their door with me in the front seat."

"I don't get it."

"Neither did I, at first. It took them at least a year to realize Charley and I weren't on the longest date ever, but actually married. We had no wedding, at least by their definition. Since they hadn't witnessed our holy union, weren't invited to take part in a big show, hadn't been able to make a big whoop-de-doo over their golden boy, they figured we were living in sin."

"Ouch."

"While Charley drove the long hauls, I spent two months in the company of people who barely exchanged a word with me. I tried to get to know them. Asked lots of questions, sought their advice. And I was sincere at the beginning, but eventually my feigned interest was too much pretense, even for me. My silence met their silence." She paused. "Then he'd come home and we'd be okay for a while."

"What did you do when he was gone?"

"Explored. Got to know the land and the river near their farm, learned to chop wood and talk to animals." Pia stood and picked up the box she'd handed me earlier. "Remember to take this home."

I went to my closet for her gift. "You, too. Merry Christmas."

"Thank you." Pia took the gift and reached for her purse. "What about New Year's? Will you be around?"

"I doubt it. School's closed 'til the third."

"I'm inviting you, like Thanksgiving. Short notice, I know. You may have other plans."

I didn't, and I would have cancelled anything for another chance to go to Pia's. I did the fake-oath thing again. "I promise to arrive sometime before midnight."

"Bring some of your music, and your Shakespeare again." Pia headed for the door. "Pack snow boots. We'll set off firecrackers," she called back from the driveway. Pia checked her watch. "Have to go now."

I opened the box right away, and found a book made with various colors of paper. The cover bore an illustration of a young woman with my features: curly brown hair, wide eyes, longish nose, plump lips. But the girl in this picture wore an expression on her face that made her beautiful and vulnerable. It took me a moment to recognize her.

Intricate ink drawings were titled in elegant script. The first page showed a sketch of my back as I stood looking out at the river bend near Pia's house. *A Visitor.* On the next page my foot crossed the threshold of her front door. *Arriving.*

There were drawings of cocktails, the parrot on the sugar cube box, a sketch of Shakespeare with characters from *The Taming of the Shrew.* She'd drawn the river, and Charley, of course, a wonderful portrait full of memory and desire. The last page had no drawing, only words. *For continuing friendship.*

Pia had brushed her pen over my heart.

Over the break, Louisville didn't get much snow, but enough freezing rain to make Mom issue a warning every time I left the house. "Better take some boots. The sidewalks might get icy. Do you have gloves? Warm up the car. Watch out, the streets are crowded this time of year." Perhaps she wouldn't have worried so if she knew I spent each day at a branch library only a few miles from home. Meeting Pia inspired me to research everything Hawaiian. History books told of beautiful islands that attracted migrants who believed they came from the taro root. Later in time, Mark Twain described paradise. James Dole planted pineapples, Don the Beachcomber invented mai-tais. But I was searching for the gods Tutu and Pia worshipped. I'd done my dance with Baptists and Episcopalians. There had to be something else for me.

In the old Hawaiian ways, one prayed upright, eyes wide open, meeting divinity straight on. Each family had special *nā àumākua*, ancestral deities, who might appear in stones and animals, in special places, and as certain people, sort of like guardian angels. That's why Pia had thanked each stone, asked pardon of low branches, and reminded each twig of its purpose. One could never be sure when these spirits would show up.

I decided to experiment. The only ancestors I knew of were my mother's Southern clan, with whom we'd lost touch. My dad came from Irish alcoholics who abandoned their children. Without relatives to invoke, I sat in my suburban home and called to sea creatures. Sharks for strength, turtles for creativity. The book Pia had made for me became my household god. I carried it with me everywhere, studying the pages several times a day. Each time I noticed another detail: a little face in a pine cone, a seashell in the river, a tiny crown on a parrot.

My parents didn't bother me as much. The focus on research and experimentation with prayer made me more tolerant of Dad's tirades. Whenever he got started, I would imagine the hand of a wise grandmother on my shoulder. Mom and I managed to cook Christmas dinner together without a single take-out dish. When Mom, Dad, and Meg bowed their heads and closed their eyes, I prayed, eyes open, looking straight ahead. "We give thanks, we seek blessing, we honor all that has come before, and all that is to come."

"Amen," we said together. When I added *mahalo*, they looked at me with surprise. There was a moment of potential, when someone could have asked, and I would have offered. But Dad lifted his bourbon, waved his glass in a mock toast, Mom said, "Please pass the potatoes," and Meg looked down at the ring from her latest boyfriend. I slumped back in my chair and picked up my fork.

New Year's Eve, I showed up at Pia's with firecrackers and two bottles of bubbly purchased by my girlfriend Susie's older brother. He made extra holiday cash buying liquor for minors. His business turned decent champagne into expensive champagne.

Following prior instructions, I walked down from the highway around nine, guided by flashlight. The house was dark. No welcoming porch light. The faint glow of the table lamp in her bedroom shone through the curtain. I knocked and waited, knocked again. I buried the bottles in the snow with the tops showing so she'd be sure to find them when she returned. Puzzled by her absence, I walked back up toward the road. Close to the highway, I heard blaring music, followed by the slam of a car door. Pia came striding around the bend.

My flashlight startled her. "Oh!" then "Hi," she said and leaned in for a hug. "I'm so sorry." She crooked her arm through mine and we headed down to her house. "Last minute errand."

I looked for a bag or box, but she carried only a purse. "She's lying," I thought, extracting the bottles from their makeshift icebox. Once inside, we poured, toasted, and played a game: Where were you on New Year's Eve of such-and-such a year? Her list included Kauai, Malibu, and Mexico. Mine, Winston-Salem, Cincinnati, and a senior class party aboard the Belle of Louisville, a paddleboat on the Ohio River. At midnight we set off strings of tiny red explosives in the snow.

Artificial lightning sparked and crackled, interrupting the vast silence.

"Resolutions," Pia said when we came back inside and plopped into the living room chairs. "You first."

I was just drunk enough to be honest: "Have sex."

"Same here." Pia laughed. "That's where I was, earlier."

"Having sex?"

"No." She paused. "I wasn't going to tell you."

"How come?"

"Afraid you'd judge me, like other women did when I took up with Charley."

"They were jealous. Not all women are like that." Dying to know the details, I made my voice confident and reassuring. "I'm not."

But Pia took the conversation elsewhere. "Sex became nearly impossible after Charley needed a wheelchair."

The frivolity of our New Year's celebration faded. Embarrassed by my lighthearted comment that opened this painful memory for her, I sat and listened.

"The first few times were awkward, but we could laugh. I was agile and creative." She smiled at a memory. "Eventually we gave up, and our relationship suffered." Pia looked down at her hands.

"How sad." I wished for better words.

"I tried to make up for the distance in a thousand ways. Wrote him little poems, baked his favorite foods, wore beautiful clothes. All that seemed to make it worse. Some months later we discovered prostate cancer the cause of our difficulties."

"Even sadder." I didn't know much about the condition, but felt her heartbreak.

"At first Charley got angry. 'I know what I'm missing, Pia. Don't tempt me.' No matter how his doctors explained the disease, Charley considered impotence his fault and thought I shouldn't be punished for his shortcomings. After months of failed attempts, he encouraged me to have sex with other men, younger men." She cleared her throat. "College boys." She got up to straighten a curtain. "I'm ready." Pia said this so matter-of-factly I thought I'd misheard her.

"Boys from my college?"

She sat down and looked at me. "Shocked?"

"Yes," I admitted. "I can't imagine guys my age would appeal to you."

"Some are more mature than others. Besides, it's more about being desired."

Now this I understood. I'd wanted Pat to want me more than anything else. Pia continued. "Remember when I was up on the campus right before Christmas break?"

I hesitated. "Yeah." My ego dropped a notch. I thought she'd come to deliver the little book.

"I was looking for Kevin Parker. You know him?"

"Everybody knows Kevin." I groaned. "And if they don't, he'll be glad to introduce himself."

"What's wrong with him?"

"He's only the most egotistical jerk in the world, that's all."

"Not true, not true." Pia shook her head in protest. "Yes, he's gorgeous. And smart. And his great-grandparents practically built the college. Parker Auditorium, Parker Stadium, Parker Drive. So add rich to that mix."

"This isn't helping me understand your point."

"Underneath he's a scared young man, with a family reputation to uphold, and no idea how to go about it. He's much more interested in art than politics, business, or any other profession his folks will choose for him."

"And you know this how?" I asked.

"I'm an artist—" she began.

"Oh my God, the book! It's incredible. Thank you." I'd written a letter, agonizing over each word, but hadn't found the courage to give it to her. My lack of expressed gratitude caused me to start mumbling. "I meant to—"

Pia raised her hand to cut me off. "I love capturing moments and pieces of moments." She hesitated. "But my art isn't a predictable income. Charley had no life insurance. His pension benefits aren't enough to cover my monthly expenses."

Unable to imagine what this had to do with Kevin Parker, I waited for her to continue.

"I don't like depending on food supplies from my California cousin. I want to go to school, college, and get an art degree. Based on my portfolio, I can get a partial scholarship, but the remaining funds aren't there."

"Your dad won't help you? Now that Charley's..."

"I haven't asked. Time for me to grow up." Pulling her shoulders back, Pia sat up straighter. "Last spring I started modeling for the Studio Art majors at the college."

"Kevin's an art major?" I managed to squeak the question over the rumble in my tiny moral universe.

"Yes, he's quite talented."

"And liked what he saw." Imagining Pia's voluptuous body, a gauzy drape flowing over her breasts, I blushed.

"I liked what he drew," Pia said. "It was the first time in a long time that I felt, well, attractive." I thought she might be defensive in the wake of my obvious judgment, but she continued without skipping a beat. "We've had coffee after class nearly every week since."

"Has he ever been here?" I didn't like the way I sounded, territorial.

"No. Not yet. Soon."

My discomfort increased. "Why now, all of a sudden?"

"I can't really answer that question. Maybe Charley's been gone long enough. It's winter. I'm lonely. Maybe it's because he'll bring in the wood. I don't know."

"He's always got girls after him. Did you know that?"

"Sure. I've seen the way they compete for his attention, but he really isn't interested. He wants to go to art school. He's got both the talent and the money."

"Maybe he's just saying that so you'll sleep with him."

"Possible, but not likely. I'm the pursuer, Laura, the one who will initiate foreplay. I actually don't think he has a clue what he's in for. Kevin called earlier and asked me out for a drink. He picked me up at the top of the hill, and we went to Maggie's. He'd been invited to several New Year's parties, but said he felt lonely."

I rolled my eyes. "You believed him? The booze must have made you crazy."

"I told him to stop by after the parties ended."

"Stop by and get laid?" I was trying to roll with the punches, stay funny without being sarcastic.

"You aren't insulted, I hope? It's just the way I am, spontaneous."

"Sorry you invited me?" Putting a mock pout on my face, I pretended to be joking.

"A little."

Sometimes I wish she wouldn't be so honest. "What should I do if he shows up?"

"Disappear." She squeezed her fingertips together, spread them into stars, as if she were a stage magician. "Poof!"

By three a.m., we were both tired. Giving up on the tryst, Pia turned out the porch light and locked the door. I went to my studio bedroom and slept without dreaming.

The next morning, when I walked into the kitchen, Kevin was making coffee. "Morning," he chirped. "Great to see you! Want a cup?"

I knew they'd had sex. No guy is that cheerful for no good reason, especially in the morning.

"Hi. Sure. Thanks."

Pia came in through the front door with an armful of firewood. So much for her fantasy about male assistance. "Kevin's made coffee," I called to her, using my told-you-so voice.

Right when I spoke, Kevin brushed past me to take the wood from Pia. He stacked the logs beside the woodstove, undamped the flue, added two pieces of pine that sizzled and sparked, waited until the air intake adjusted, closed the door. "We'll be nice and warm soon, ladies."

"Thank you," Pia said in her told-you-so voice.

Gallant and gorgeous, handsome in an unusual way, Kevin had an athlete's body without the stockiness of the football jocks. He ran track and swam. Longish dark hair and bright blue eyes made a great combination. Chiseled features made him more man than boy. I had to leave before I wanted to have sex with him. My mind worked on an excuse, but there was no place to go, since school was still closed for the holiday. Maybe I'd think of something while gathering my belongings from the studio.

"Hey," Kevin said. "Don't leave before breakfast." He turned over a perfect omelet. "*Voila!*" He set a plate in front of each of us.

"You cook?" The words flew from my mouth with a nasty tone.

"Only dish I know how to make. Thank *Tante* Annette who spent a summer at *Cordon Bleu.*"

Pia caught my eye and suppressed a giggle. Only Kevin Parker would have an aunt who attended cooking school in Paris. After we ate and traded standard pleasantries, Kevin started asking questions. "Why the English major when theology's your passion?"

"'Whatever does a woman do with a theology degree?'"

"Parents want you to be a teacher, right?"

"Oh, yeah. Safe profession for a woman, summers off. All that good stuff."

"At the beginning of my junior year I declared a Poli/Sci major." His mouth turned down in distaste. "One miserable semester reading Talleyrand and Machiavelli." Looking at Pia, his face shifted back to handsome. "Last spring I switched to Studio Art."

"Are there jobs in the field?" I sounded like my own parents.

"I won't ever need a job." He smiled. "After graduation I get a couple of years to be like everybody else. Then I inherit." He didn't brag, merely stated fact. "Trust funder." He stood up from the table.

"What will you do with the money?" I imagined he'd build a Playboy mansion, complete with an art studio. His paintings of nudes would hang in the hallways.

He pulled his shoulders back and spoke his best Boston Brahmin. "We Pah-kahs have our charities. Old money will nev-ah, ev-ah run out." Then he became Kevin again. "I'll be required to serve on boards and speak at fundraisers. I'll actually have to research our causes, because Dad forbids hiring speech writers."

"You'll both have adult responsibilities soon enough," Pia said. "Don't wish your lives away."

After we cleaned the kitchen together, Pia got out her sketchbook and began a charcoal drawing of Kevin while he sat, cross-legged, on one of the overstuffed chairs. Winter sunlight streamed into the living room. It was one of life's rare moments when everything was beautiful. He'd brought a *Beatles* record, their first Christmas message to US fans, and we listened to Tiny Tim playing *Nowhere Man* on the ukulele.

"Beats Nat King Cole any day." I wasn't trying to be sarcastic, I only wanted to tease Pia about her age, but the comment came out wrong and the mood was broken.

Kevin cleared his throat and got up to put more wood on the fire. "I'm going now," he announced. He reached for his coat and walked over to Pia. He examined the sketch. "Doesn't do me justice." For a moment I couldn't tell if he was serious, but he winked, then bent down to give Pia a quick kiss. "See you tonight, ladies. And I'm bringing a friend." He looked at me and wiggled his eyebrows Groucho-style. I tried to hate him.

The minute he was out the door I had a meltdown. "My hair's a mess, I didn't bring any decent clothes or make up, even. What will I talk about?" I paced. "I wonder who it is. Kevin's a senior! And he pals around with other cool guys. But everybody's off campus now. What if he brings a townie?"

"Relax." Pia placed a hand on my arm. "We've got the day. Let me work on your hair and makeup." Cupping my chin in her hand, she turned my face, her blank canvas, from side to side. Then she stepped back to study my pants and sweater. "Hmm, let's check out my closet."

"Just let me leave."

"No way. New Year's Resolution, remember?"

"The rule is you have a day to take it back. I'm not ready, not ready at all for this."

"Sure you are, honey." She gave me a hug.

Fixing my hair took longer than preparing dinner. The unruly curls were winter-frizzy. They kept popping up like corkscrews through layers of hair spray. Pia insisted on trimming the top and didn't let me look until she finished.

"Gee, thanks. I look like Little Orphan Annie." I pouted at my reflection. "Only not red-headed, freckled, five years old, or cute."

"Stop being so critical. You look pretty. Let's use some make up on you."

I sat still for another forty-five minutes. And when she turned me around to face the mirror, I saw an older, more sophisticated me, the face I would grow into, not half bad.

"Okay," I said. "That works."

"Let's get you into some of my clothes. We're about the same size."

"Stop being diplomatic, your breasts are bigger than mine."

She laughed. "Nothing a good push up bra can't fix."

The fashion transformation succeeded as well. By early evening I wore a flowing silk tunic, printed with reddish orange poppies, over a pair of my own tight blue jeans. My eyes, accented by smoky eye shadow, seemed darker than usual. Thick brunette curls gently flipped and flopped over the crown of my head. A few stray strands fell across my brow. The lips, plumped with liner, were dark-ish tan.

Pia stood behind me at the floor length mirror. "*Voila!* Like Kevin's omelet. You look special and delicious. Can you see the difference?"

"My dad always claimed he was black Irish." The planes of my face carried the genes of western Ireland. Made up, I looked less like my Southern grandmother, more like my Dad's mom and sisters.

"It must be true." Pia brushed her own hair, pulled it back with a headband, and said, "Let's make dinner."

We cooked and sang. It snowed more. We stoked the fire. Kevin didn't show. I was relieved, but Pia worried. After we ate and shared a bottle of wine, we curled up under blankets and fell asleep in the living room chairs. Near dawn the cold woke us. Pia took a look at me and smirked. I headed for the bathroom. My eye makeup drifted; my hair buzzed with static electricity. The silkiness of the tunic drooped. My top half looked like a wrinkled flower bed.

Around six Kevin arrived, alone. As he came up the walk I headed for the studio, figuring his explanation would require privacy.

"Hel-lo," I called loudly, before entering late morning. "Come in. It's safe, he's gone." Pia stood at the stove, her back to me. I noticed both the gentle curve of her neck and the relaxation in her shoulders.

"You did it again, right?"

She turned around. "Sometimes I don't get you, Laura. You want to be my friend, yet you come up with these little digs suggesting I'm old, and downright immoral. Am I disappointing you in some way?"

"Sorry." I shook my head. "I'm confused, that's all." I sat at the kitchen table. "And frustrated. All semester I've pushed boys off, literally. We pet up to the brink, I refuse. I'm evicted from a steamy car and end up walking home with my underpants in my pocket."

"At least you have the foresight not to leave your underwear in their cars." She tried to coax a smile from me.

"Guys talk about sex as if it were a sport. 'First base, and so on,' 'Did ya score?' Tell me it's more than a contest."

"You can do the physical deed with anybody, but chemistry counts."

"The harder I try, the more I end up feeling like a jerk. I'm no good at primping and don't know how to flirt."

Pia stood behind me and gently touched my shoulders. "Exude confidence."

"No one ever showed me how."

"*Wahine* energy." She hulaed a little circle around me, her hips in fluid motion, arms playful, beckoning. "Come on. Every woman's got a bit of temptress in her."

"Like your sister-in-law? She's about your age, right? Do you really think you have anything in common with her, sexually?"

"Maybe she dared to wear a see-through negligee, once." We both smiled at the image this provoked. Sturdy, stuffy Janet, clad in diaphanous material, carrying her satchel.

"But you've got everything figured out. You're experienced. Beautiful." Each word came out sounding like an accusation.

"Laura, I don't…" Pia gave me one of her direct soul searching stares, "… have anything figured out. My world went upside down when Charley died. We were married for nearly as long as you've been alive. I'm making all this up as I go along. Don't punish me for something you've only imagined."

"Okay." I nodded. "Sorry."

"Sex is frustrating and confusing for everybody." Pia, signaling end-of-subject, folded her arms.

"What does Kevin want?" Determined to persist, I raised my voice. "Other than sex?"

"Hard to say. Maybe to be taken seriously by an adult. He's tentative and wants to please."

"That sounds kind of nice."

"It is, for now." She wasn't looking at me anymore.

"Because the relationship can't really go anywhere?"

"Right. He'll graduate. I'll go to art school." She shrugged. "Life happens."

"Wish mine would." I stood up. "I've got to get back up the hill, to the ivory tower and all."

I paused, waiting for Pia to say "Don't go" or "Come back next weekend," but instead she said, "Okay, bye." She gave me a little squeeze before she picked up her sketchbook. "Take care," she added, lifting her pen.

As before, leaving without any promise of return made me nervous. Like Kevin, I needed Pia more than she needed me. For all I knew the next time the Backbone would be clear enough to walk, Pia would be enrolled in art school God-knows-where. The tension in my gut grew in proportion to each step I took toward Highway 97. Just when I decided to turn back, to fabricate something I'd forgotten, a silver van slowed and stopped.

"Hey. Hello," the driver said as he rolled down his window. Pushing his face forward, he let out a giant breath, testing the cold. "Wow." He pulled his head back into the cab. "Winter, huh?" He was wearing a Grateful Dead T-shirt and the van bore California plates. Before I could say anything, he slipped on a glove and stuck his hand out the window. My mitten met his glove, my eyes met his, and I knew he must be Pia's food-bearing cousin. He was absolutely adorable. "Nakoa." He paused. "Nick."

"Laura." My teeth chattered.

"You go to the college, I bet."

Shifting from one foot to another to keep warm, I nodded.

"Know Pia, I bet." He kept shaking my hand.

"Right again."

"Only one thing wrong with this picture." His voice, deep and warm, took the edge off my chill.

"And that is?" I dropped my hand to adjust my backpack.

"We're going in opposite directions." He leaned across and opened the passenger door. "Hop in."

I hesitated.

"Oh, come on! It's cold. I'll turn the van around in Pia's driveway and take you back to school."

I marched around the van and climbed up into the cab.

"Aloha." Nick's voice made the word mean everything it could: *hello, good-bye, love.* What have you and my cousin been up to?" His skin was a shade browner than Pia's, and I could see the resemblance in his dark eyes and full mouth. Like Pia, he charmed me. Not as old as she, but way too old for me. "We, uh, celebrated New Year's here." I was tongue tied.

"Guess what? We did the same in California!" He laughed, poking fun at me and amused at his own cleverness. He pulled into Pia's drive, honked and waved at the front windows, reversed, and drove toward the highway. "I'll be on campus Saturday. How about I pick you up around dinnertime and you can spend the rest of your weekend with Pia and me?" As he spoke, Nick ran his large hand over my knees. Affectionate, exploring, definitely sexual. He had removed the glove.

"Sure." I positioned my backpack in my lap to discourage further groping, and my heart did a little victory dance. I'd get to see Pia again soon.

He dropped me off at the edge of campus. "I'd walk you, but my coat's stuffed in the cargo bin." He gestured toward the boxes in the back of the van.

"That's okay. I'm used to it."

"Aloha, Laura." He blew me a kiss.

Still charmed, I indulged in a vague fantasy involving sex with Nick. An older man would know all about pleasing a woman, and I could tell he was interested. But any relationship with him might impact mine with Pia, and I didn't want to take that chance. Besides, he lived far away, and I yearned for a constant lover.

As the school week unfolded, I spotted Nick a few times near the Student Union. Once, his van was parked behind Fraternity Row. If I started asking questions about Nick, I couldn't keep Pia a secret. Ear to the ground, I overheard a girl in one of my classes bragging about the pot she smoked the night before. "Some guy from California sold powerful weed to Janine. He's older, really cool. I'm meeting him for drinks next weekend. Wheeler-dealer."

I kicked myself for being so naïve. The pantry must contain their stash. That would explain the harried phone calls. And the fact that everybody got dropped off at the top of the hill. What had she said? She and Charley had planned it that way? Pot was just making an appearance on our provincial little Midwestern campus. I'd heard about Mary Jane, but hadn't tried any, didn't know anyone who got stoned, at least, no one who admitted it.

By the time Nick picked me up Saturday night, I'd worried myself sick. Literally. He tried to get touchy-feely with me again, but stopped when I sneezed. As soon as we came in the front door, Pia walked toward me for a hug. "Better not get too close." I coughed. "I'm sick."

"Ginger tea, then." Pia went into nurse mode, directing Nick to put the kettle on. She turned one of the big chairs toward the wood stove. "Sit." She wrapped a crocheted afghan around my shoulders. I let her coddle me.

Nick brought the tea. "Fresh ginger root, with honey. Tutu swore by it when we were kids."

"Oh, that's right, Nick," Pia said. "Remember when you didn't want to march in the Kamehameha parade? You were about thirteen and you were supposed to play the French horn, but you were concerned a certain *ku `uipo* might make fun of you, so—"

"Clarinet," Nick interrupted.

"Anyway…," Pia looked at me and I could see she really wanted me to understand, to get an idea of their grandmother and a glimpse into their youth. "…you pretended to have a cold. Tutu told me to put cayenne pepper in your ginger tea, 'If he's so hot for this sweetheart, we'll watch him breathe fire!' You didn't even take a sip. Just the steam coming off that cup got you to band practice early." The cousins smiled at the memory.

"Tutu, of the most darling laugh and brightest eyes." Nick said. "Just like our Pia."

I was half listening, half plotting. All week I'd thought of ways to confront her. I planned to be accusatory as well as morally indignant. First, I would point out her errors in judgment, then advise her of possible consequences. But I didn't want Nick around. When he left to "meet a girl for drinks" I was both relieved and nervous.

"I'm getting a couple of hot water bottles for your bed," Pia said.

"Before you do that, I need—" I started.

"More tea? Are you warm enough? Let's get another log on the fire." She moved toward the stove.

"Stop. I need to tell you something."

"Oh, goody." Pia, ignoring my warnings, came close, and perched on the edge of my chair, practically in my lap. "Gossip."

"Not goody. I'm so upset I've made myself sick."

"Did Nick make a pass at you? It wouldn't surprise me."

"Yes. Twice. My cold kept me safe this time. I'm flattered, actually, but not really interested. He's a little old for me. I-I mean—"

"That's okay," Pia laughed. "No offense taken. What's wrong?"

"I hear he's selling pot on campus."

"That's true." Pia responded matter-of-factly. "What else?"

"Nothing. I just thought maybe you should consider the risk, that's all."

"Believe me, I have. For almost ten years."

"Pot's been around that long?" The surprise in my voice made her smile. "At Hanover?"

"Not just pot. Bennies, pain pills, and anything else that will get you high or knock you out."

Looking into her face, the way she so often studied me, I launched into the interrogation I'd rehearsed. "Don't you think it's wrong to sell drugs to college kids?"

"Of course, I do. I think the whole thing stinks. That's why I'm not involved."

"Not involved?" My voice relaxed.

"Charley and Nick put the drug business together after Charley's accident. Nicky hadn't really found his calling. And he lives up in the Bay Area. California's youth culture is light years ahead of Indiana's." Pia paced as she spoke. "They got the idea one day when my husband refused his pain pill. Said the drug made him anxious. Nick, on the other hand, washed down a double dose and enjoyed the experience. Charley asked his doctors for more medications, different kinds for various types of pain. The guys got their stash practically free."

"And after that?"

"Nick took the money he made from peddling pills and added pot to the inventory. At first he took the drugs back to the Bay Area, but the last few years he realized he had a built-in clientele in the college kids. Suddenly Nick had a job and Charley made extra money that he put into an account for me." Pia explained each step of the operation as if it made perfect sense. "But, guess what?" She put her hand to her forehead in mock surprise. "When Charley died, the pill pipeline ran dry."

"But Nick didn't stop."

Pia moved toward the wood stove. "Nope. He's expanding. Raising prices. Getting his pills on the street." Adding a log to the fire, she closed the stove door with an angry slam. "He's hounding me to take the seller's role. Save him the trouble."

"You said you weren't involved."

"Not by choice. I don't use or sell drugs. But the last few months Nicky's been unloading his stash, disguised as fancy foods, in—"

"And storing them in your pantry." Excited to be right about something, finally, I felt my illness retreat. "I thought so." My voice rang with triumph.

"Not so fast, Nancy Drew." Pia shook her head. "You don't know the details, and were mighty wrong about me."

"Yes, I was. I apologize. Really."

"Accepted. But take note. Here's some advice from an older woman: put me on a pedestal, and I'll have too far to fall. I know. Because that's what I did to Charley. I was an inexperienced, love-struck nineteen-year-old girl when he walked into my life. I don't regret our marriage for a moment, but the man disappointed me in ways I could not have imagined." Pia had tears in her voice. "Sermon over," she said.

When we were both done sniffling, I asked for more tea. "Speaking of sermons," I paused to take a sip, "I was ready to give you one."

"I'm sure you were. But please spare me. I've had enough judgment to last a lifetime and then some. What I'm looking for here is pure, uncomplicated friendship." She paused. "Do you think there is such a thing?"

"I don't know." Philosophizing on the subject of friendship was beyond my experience. "I hope so."

"My lifestyle shocks you sometimes."

"Am I that obvious?"

"Yes. And you're totally forgiven. I don't depend on your approval."

"I want yours."

Her smile told me she'd known that already. "I'm in over my head, fooling myself." Pia returned to sit on the arm of the chair. "The drugs are here, in my house. Law enforcement will never let that go. Guilty as charged. There goes my life." She held out her wrists for imaginary hand cuffs. "Maybe you can help me think of something."

"Really?" I sat up straighter.

"At Thanksgiving I took canned goods to a food drive at the Presbyterian church up the road."

"I remember. While I fixed the leftovers."

"What if we dumped some canned goods in donation bins? Spread them out at soup kitchens? Somebody's bound to open something, pills or pot, and alert the authorities."

"There'd be no way to track it, right?" The plan made me nervous.

"Right. An article in the paper might convince Nick to forego the food ruse."

"Sounds too simple."

"You're right. He's stubborn, enough little boy in him to thumb his nose at the system. The threat of getting busted would only excite him."

Warm from the fire and the tea, I stood. As the afghan slipped to the floor, my foot caught the blanket and a kick sent it into the chair. I took the graceful move as an omen for good luck. "We're getting rid of the drugs. Now." My decisiveness surprised us both.

Pia nodded. I followed her to the kitchen. We worked without words. She stood inside the pantry and handed me the cans and jars, a bucket brigade of contraband. In a short time, we filled a half dozen brown paper sacks. "Let's drive up the hill," I said. "We're about to make some frat boys really happy."

Grabbing our coats, we bundled up and dashed through the cold to the car. It took ten minutes for the ice on the windshield to melt. Despite the blasting fan of the defroster, our rapid breaths kept fog on the windows. Once they cleared, Pia drove fast. She took the curving dirt road up to the highway at a speed that made the bags tip sideways, causing cans to spill onto the floor. Intending to restore order, I climbed over the back seat and picked up a leaky jar. My hands became instantly sticky. "Pull over for a sec," I instructed. She turned on the dome light. "The label says 'Fruit Cocktail.'" Feeling adventurous, I took a bite of a syrupy peach half. "Want some?" When Pia turned around, I pushed a gooey red cherry into her mouth.

Waiting for a rush that never came, we got the giggles. "Guess we goofed, must have grabbed the wrong jar." She found napkins in the glove compartment, and I wiped my hands. And then all the air went out of our plan. "We may not be high. Just crazy." Pia groaned. "We ditch the drugs, then what?"

Embarrassed to admit that I hadn't really thought things through, I scrambled into the front seat. "We don't know. Yet."

"If we dump them on campus, Nick will know pretty close to immediately. Then he'll demand I repay him the value."

"Pia, listen," I started, "when Nick gets back tonight tell him you're leaving town next weekend. Ask for a loan."

"For what?"

"Make something up. Say you want to take an art class in Bloomington, at the University of Indiana. An illustrator from *Atlantic Monthly* is taking on a few select students." I was on a roll.

"Go on."

"You submitted a portfolio and were thrilled to be chosen. But you didn't count on the expenses associated with the trip. Gas, food, hotel." The more details I added, the more we believed it ourselves.

Pia turned the car around and headed back down the hill.

"Tell him you'll take the entire stash to sell up north."

"He'll want profits."

"When he gets back. Gives us a few months to come up with another story."

"But what's the money for?" she asked.

"Buying time."

As soon as we reached the house, we unloaded and restocked the pantry. We made everything look as it was before Nick left. I sat in the chair by the fire, crumpled a few tissues in my lap, and draped the afghan over my shoulders. Pia made more tea. We whispered, even though there was no reason to. "So, what happens when I get to IU with a car full of drugs?" Pia asked.

I corrected her: "When *we* get to IU."

"Okay."

"We drive straight to the university and drop the bags. The campus is huge, no one will ever be able to trace the stuff."

We heard Nick's van. "Let's hope he doesn't notice your car windows aren't covered with ice," I said. "Or that the engine's still warm."

"He won't. Usually he can't resist getting stoned. 'Quality control,' he calls it. He'll want to eat." Pia went to the kitchen. Sure enough Nick came in, relaxed, goofy, and hungry.

"How was your date?" I asked.

"Oh, super. College girls are so smart and funny."

"Are you being sarcastic?"

"A little. She isn't even twenty-one. Having a drink involves buying a bottle, then sitting in the van with the engine running. Takes the fun out, know what I mean?"

"Sure do, I'm a minor."

"Now look who's sarcastic." He made a fist and gave my upper arm a gentle punch.

"Maybe you shouldn't hang out with college girls." Trying to looking superior, I raised my nose in the air. "Or college boys, for that matter. Pick on people your own age."

"Hey, who are you, Dean of Student Affairs?" Even though Nick tried to keep his tone light, I could tell he wasn't really joking. He was smart enough to wonder if Pia had told me about the drugs.

"Pia's in the kitchen. Let's go see what she's making." The diversion worked. We spent the rest of the evening eating chow mein and talking about movies. I went out to the studio before they retired. Nick waved. "Nighty-night." Hoping Pia would lay the groundwork for Bloomington, I blew her a kiss and tried to say everything with my eyes.

Nick bought the story. Before heading back to northern California he loaned Pia five hundred dollars. The following weekend, Pia and I reloaded the food cans and set out for the two-hour drive to IU. In spite of the danger, or, perhaps, because of the tension, we laughed about our stopgap measure. I introduced Pia to "my music" on the car radio: "Love Child," "Hey Jude," "I Heard It Through The Grapevine." We sang along in decent harmony.

In broad daylight, we left our groceries in a parking lot near the Commons. Each bag appeared to be overflowing with albacore tuna tins, or canned coconut milk, or bamboo shoots.

"No one will report their score," Pia said as we put down the last sack. "Money will be made and good times will be had."

"A part of me wishes we could find out what happens."

"Tell that part to forget." She wagged her finger toward me. "Wipe your mind clean of the whole trip. Tutu taught me not to leave a psychic trail. Someone might follow."

"I'm not sure I understand."

"Doesn't matter. We're creating a campus legend. They'll tell this story for years to come. Maybe not to their children, but to each other. The Drug Fairy."

Glad to be rid of our cargo, we both laughed. Pia pulled three small spotted objects from her coat pocket. "I almost forgot." Placing them on the ground, in a circle, she fussed with each one until satisfied with their position. "Cowrie shells," she said when she saw the question on my face, "so no one gets hurt." She promised to explain later.

On the way home, Pia drove with tense shoulders, and I spent the first half hour staring out the back windshield to see if cops had followed. Turning forward, I fiddled with the radio dial, but Pia swatted my hand away. "Hey," I said, "did I tell you about my big theology assignment?"

"Nope." Pia didn't sound interested.

I launched into a nervous monologue. "We're supposed to use three creation myths to construct our own religion. No Judeo-Christian, Greco-Roman, or Norse folklore allowed. Prof says they're too similar. We grew up influenced by those beliefs, but don't even know it. Like fish don't know they swim in water."

Her hands gripped the wheel. "Oh."

"Remember when you asked if I believed in evil?"

Eyes on the road, she gave a slight nod.

"Well, I did some research and found out the Cherokees have no concept of Satan."

The comment got her attention. "The devil scares me." Pia shuddered. "When Christians came to old Hawaii they made one up. *Kanaloa* was a god of the sea and guide to the underworld. Magic, for sure, but not evil."

"The Cherokees solve the problem entirely. Simply don't believe in evil, and it can't exist, at least not in a personal way."

"That's a relief."

"Also," I went on, finding comfort in reciting facts, "the Maya believe humans came from maize. A much better start than Original Sin."

As we pulled into the driveway, Pia nodded. "Hawaiians trace their ancestry back to *kalo*, taro root."

"Does the old religion have a name?"

"None that I know of. *Kahuna* translates both as 'priest' and 'sorcerer.' That ought to tell you something." When we got out of the car, Pia looked around, as if expecting Nick, or law enforcement. "I'm not native, you know, not even a full blood." She unlocked the front door. "Most everything I know comes from Tutu, and she didn't explain much. Everything may not be exactly true."

"That's okay. Tell me anyway?"

We went inside, made a light supper, and Pia began to talk. I sat, taking notes, while she walked back and forth across the living room. Her hands moved along with the story, and I had a hard time keeping my eyes on the page. "Why the cowries?" Dismissing my first question with a wave of her hand and two words: "goddess protection," she launched into her narrative. "My grandmother was born on Kauai, the Garden Isle, only two generations after *kapu* ended."

A student at a lecture, I wrote the word with no idea of its meaning.

"Codes of conduct that governed lifestyle, politics, the legal system. You name it. Strict gender taboos regulated society. Men did all the cooking and prepared women's meals in a separate oven. Any meal containing pork, bananas, taro, or coconut was shared only among men. Mind you, these were staples."

"Seems kind of harsh."

"*Hā' oles* can't understand."

"Who?"

Pia walked over to me, touched her nose to mine, inhaled. She motioned for me to share her breath. "*Honi.*" She stepped back. "A native greeting unknown to foreigners. *Hā' ole* means 'without breath.' Islanders thought the newcomers were without spirit. Dead."

I continued to write.

"You're one. No offense. So was my dad. And Charley, of course. *Kapu* had merit and made sense in their culture. Certain native foods build the feminine spirit, others nourish the masculine." Pia walked around the back of my chair and looked over my shoulder. When she saw my sketch of a banana, next to a shape that was supposed to be a pork chop, she laughed, then resumed pacing in front of me. "Influences from afar changed those laws, and one simple gesture brought the old ways to an end."

"What happened?"

"Kamehameha the Great shared a meal with his mother and the women of his court."

"Can you spell his name for me?" My pencil kept moving.

She waved her hand. "Just put a 'K.'"

"I've already got one for the island. Don't know how to spell that either."

"Is it really important?"

Sorry to have interrupted her train of thought, I shook my head. "When was this?"

She thought for a moment. "Mid eighteen-hundreds."

"Okay." I made a note in the margin.

"Missionaries arrived soon after. They outlawed the old religion and banned public performances of *hula*. Leave it to the men of God. Only it didn't end there," she went on, "Most family groups, including my grandmother's, kept some of the old taboos and disregarded others. But they worshipped a new 'only begotten Son of God.'" Pia lifted her hands to the heavens and clasped them together, as if in prayer. "Tutu liked Jesus well enough, she didn't hold with the part that He alone could save one's soul. She taught me that many gods dwell in many things."

"I like that."

"Me, too." Pia asked to read my notes. Satisfied that I'd gotten her ideas down, she nodded and closed my notebook. "Enough religion for one night. Let's clean up."

Thinking about how Nick might react when he discovered we dumped the drugs, I stayed awake. I studied the walls in the studio, wishing myself into the paintings, eager for an escape into paradise, then got out of bed and rummaged through Pia's craft cabinet. Happy to find a stash of cowrie shells, I placed them in a circle on the floor. The small spotted half-eggs would have to work overtime. Goddess protection. Superstition or not, the ritual comforted me.

In the morning Pia came into the studio with a tray. Tea steamed from green cups made to look like palm fronds. "Charley's mom gave us these." She perched on the edge of the bed. We sipped.

"What's she like, Charley's mom?" I asked.

"Mama tried to smooth things over with the family. Nothing was ever said, but she gave us things, like the chairs Charley grew up with and these cups, which she bought at a flea market. She thought they 'would remind me of home.'"

"I'm sure she didn't mean to sound patronizing."

"She's a Midwestern farm wife. Anything foreign terrifies her, especially her son's wife."

"But she had years to get to know you."

"We connected now and then, but never grew close." Pia finished her tea, then picked up our conversation from the night before.

I reached for my notebook, but she shook her head.

"In order to understand the old religion, you have to recognize the meaning of hula."

I snuggled under the covers, a child about to hear her bedtime story in the morning.

"Tutu's father worked as a sugar wholesaler for Grove Farm." Pia went into lecture mode again. "She and her brothers attended school with the Wilcox children, whose family owned the estate. Tutu's father didn't want her to marry an Islander."

"Even though he was one?"

"Correct. It was rare for a Kauian to hold such a high position. His family's social status had risen."

"Men really do run everything."

"Up to a point. Peter Denman, my grandfather, an investor from New Hampshire, visited Grove Farm when he was a young man. He fell in love. Not only with the old ways, but also with Noelani, the wholesaler's beautiful teenage daughter. Said he 'couldn't see straight for the rest of his life.' They married in 1912 and remained on Kauai. Tutu taught him her language and the hula."

"A man can hula?" I smiled, trying to picture it.

"Both my grandparents knew several dances as well as the chants."

"What about your mother? Did she follow the old ways?"

"Right after they married, Dad brought Mom from Kauai to California. At first they settled in San Ramon, near Aunt Tina, who kept Island customs."

"Nick's mom."

Pia nodded. "Right around the time Mom became pregnant, my parents moved to Palo Alto, where Island ways paled in comparison to being a faculty wife at Stanford. Mom changed her Hawaiian name. *Alika* became Alice, in every way."

"You ended up in the white world."

"Yes. In Tutu's eyes Mom committed the worst of transgressions. By denying her Polynesian heritage, Mom pissed off her ancestors, to say nothing of the family spirits."

"Did Tutu and Alice ever make peace?"

"When I was born, Tutu saw the chance for redemption. She cultivated my Hawaiian side. To her credit, she never spoke derisively about any *haole*. She would say things like, 'Oh, the Irish have their dancing and their songs, too' before she would teach me a chant and movement."

Smiling at the image of an upright Irish jig beside the fluid sway of hula, I asked Pia to demonstrate. She removed her socks and stood at the foot of the bed. The backdrop of the murals made the setting realistic. Even without music, the flow of her hands, hips, and feet became song. Looking nothing like the hula girls in travel catalogues or in the movies, Pia wore a flannel nightgown and moved across the floor like water. The beauty of the dance lingered in the room. She invoked something I could almost touch.

"A glimpse of ancient hula," she said, catching her breath. "Let me tell you another story." She sat on the floor and didn't wait for my permission. "You can't see this particular dance except in a handful of schools on Kauai. Tourists never see *kahiko*, which tells stories of the gods and goddesses. Students were secluded lest they make a mistake and displease the deities.

"That's where Tutu learned the nuance of movement." Pia stretched her legs out in front of her. Tiny muscles in her feet pulsed. "Right fourth toe pointing west dedicates the dance to Teave, a creation god. On the left we're invoking Lady Ra, His daughter. Hula dancers create weather. Sweat is rain; breath, wind; heartbeat, thunder." Pia reached for her socks. "Native islanders consider their bodies an extension of land and nature."

"Sounds like you spent a lot of time with your grandmother."

"Tutu was my lifeline, Kauai, my reward, the only way I survived childhood in California. 'Get good grades, do chores, attend Sunday school, spend the summer at Grove Farm.'"

"You were lucky. No old ways in my veins, no wise ancestors to pass down the knowledge of the gods."

"Don't worry, Laura." Pia stood and picked up the tray. "My spiritual boat's pretty crowded. You can have some of mine."

Throughout the winter our frequent weekend visits kept me in high spirits. We hiked, weather permitting, discovering tiny fish swimming under broken ice in thawing creeks. We played games counting animal tracks and bird calls. When we got back, she would sketch; I would write. Our journal grew.

Time at Pia's house removed me from the loop of campus social life. Often I wondered how I was going to keep my New Year's resolution to enter the world of the sexually initiated. Pia was certainly keeping hers. On Saturday nights, when Kevin showed up, I put on my boots and trudged back up the hill to an empty house. My roommates would be out on dates or off campus.

In early March, Pia decided we should create a list of desirable attributes for my beloved. "Let's call him forward," she said, pen in hand. "He can't find you if your voice is too weak."

"How about tall? Can he be tall?"

"Laura, the physical package isn't important. Think about character."

"It's important to me." I crossed my arms in protest. "Sexy. Write it down."

She did. "Anything else?"

"Like what?"

"You want him to be honest, don't you? Kind? Happy?" Pia kept writing, adding whatever she wanted to the list. Then we went outside to her flower garden where tiny hyacinths grew along the border. She tore the list into miniscule bits and urged them under the dark soil with her fingers. "Take some."

"It looks like confetti." A sudden strong breeze carried tiny pieces from my cupped hand up and out past the wood pile. As soon as I started after them, Pia took my arm. "The wind god's blessing you."

One morning I noticed an empty coffee cup in the kitchen sink, and knew Pia was up, but couldn't find her anywhere. Outside I placed a hand on the hood of her car. Cold. Maybe Kevin picked her up, or maybe they were walking. But my internal radar kept giving off disturbing signals. What if Nick had returned? I walked to the river and looked in all directions. Over the chirping of robins came a faint human sound, something between a cry and a song.

Spring growth made seeing through the trees difficult, but my ears led me to a small clearing. Propped on one knee, Pia held an object over her head with both hands. The gesture was one of supplication; the chant, plaintive. Sensing my presence, she lowered her hands, touched the object to her forehead, then placed it on the ground. Her slow, deliberate movements suggested a practiced ritual. "Come here." She beckoned with one hand. Her voice sounded soft, but not strained, even though she'd been singing for several minutes. She patted the ground, a spot soft with new spring grass. I sat. We listened to bird-chirps until she spoke. The bundle, covered with royal blue cloth, was tied with twine, crisscrossing in three large X's. "Go ahead, touch."

"I'm not sure I want to. What's inside?"

"Amulets. Special shells, *tapa* cloth, feathers."

"Where did they come from?"

"Tutu. Traditional bundles contain spirits of ancestors, living beings, or both." Cradling the bundle as if it were a baby, Pia moved it into her lap.

"Maybe the better question is *who's* in there?"

"I'm not sure. My grandmother calls this a *keiki mana*, a child with spiritual power. My connection to her and vice versa, like a walkie-talkie." Her eyes looked past me at something I couldn't see.

"What were you singing?"

"*Waiho kēnā i ke akua*, take it to the gods." Lifting the spirit child, she repeated the chant several times, and then held the bundle out to me. I gave the cloth a tentative pat.

"Go on back to the house now." She stood. "I'll be along in a minute."

Along the way I wondered where the bundle lived and how often she contacted the spirits. What was she taking to the gods? And which gods?

Pia had been worrying about Nick, avoiding his calls either by not answering the incessant rings or inventing emergencies. "The pipes are about to freeze!" she would shout or, "The house is filling with smoke," or "The wood truck's in the driveway." She talked me into answering more than once. "Lying doesn't come easily to me. It drains my *mana*."

What difference would it make if a haole was deceitful? Pia must have thought I had precious little life spirit to drain. I became an adept liar: "Pia's out running errands, working in the studio, in bed with a cold." All the while she would be miming "hang up" and mouthing "bye." I had to work to keep laughter out of my voice.

When the weather turned warm for good, Pia painted the window sills soft yellow. She polished the maple cabinets from shiny to lustrous. Flower garden plots appeared, outlined by tiny grey river stones. "The house is my biggest art project," she announced. Like everything, she was bursting with vitality.

April meant spring break, but still no boyfriend for me to play with. I wanted to take Pia to Louisville. Not because I wanted to share my family with her, but with the hope that she could contact my ancestors on my behalf. Perhaps a spiritual connection could transform my parents' behavior. But before I could ask, she reminded me about Angel Falls. "It's the best time of year to go," she said. "Not too hot yet. Rolling green hills. Lush."

"Yes." I found myself always saying yes to Pia.

"Fair warning," she added, "we'll have to visit the Draper farm. Obligatory."

"Maybe you should go alone."

"You've got to be kidding. You're my buffer."

"So that's why you want me to go?"

"Well, that's one reason."

"Give me another." Sarcasm crept into my voice. "Please do."

"The beauty of the river. Native American dwellings. Drape's childhood home. I want to share those with you. It's certainly not a duty."

"Sorry for the tone." I paused. "It's just that our friendship feels so lopsided. You have so much to share."

"And you don't?"

"Not really."

"Laura." Facing me, Pia rested her hands on my shoulders. "You have listened to me pour my heart out over Charley. You read Shakespeare with me. You write our adventures and take risks. You respect my culture. Most importantly, you let me be exactly who I am. Do you know what a gift that is? What a relief?"

"You, exactly who you are, are exceptional."

"A lot of people think I'm a freak." Pia made a monster face and growled.

"Well, you are a little weird." I smiled. "Tell you what. I'll be your buffer, you be mine. We'll go to Louisville first, stay a day or two, and meet my family, then head upriver." The words sounded fine, but my gut clenched with anxiety. My parents wouldn't know what to do with Pia. They might find her amusing at best. Mom would whisper to me behind her back, "Laura, is she Christian?" Dad might be capable of some smiling-and-nodding before he fell into his alcohol dreams. My sister Meg would think Pia was cool, but she'd be out the door within half an hour.

"Okay, sounds good."

"Never mind." I shook my head. "If I go for the weekend and invent an excuse to return, we can still make the trip to Angel Falls."

My quick visit to Louisville brought no surprises, and I couldn't wait to get back to Indiana. When I returned, Pia was standing out front. "Nick's back."

"He must be upset."

"Understatement of the year. I need to go away for a while."

"Take me with you." I didn't care where.

Pia shook her head. "Tutu's asking for me."

"What do you mean?"

"To go to Kauai."

"She's alive?"

"You're surprised?"

"I assumed she inhabited the land of the ancestors, deceased. Maybe because all of my grandparents have died."

"Well, Tutu's an ancestor, all right. She'll never let you forget that, but now she's got a bad hip. Last week she fell off a horse. She's asked Nick to install bars in the shower, maybe a ramp to her door. She wants him to bring me along. I'm sure she knows about the drug business."

"Did Nick tell her?"

"No one needs to tell Tutu anything, she just knows. Maybe not all the details, but the gist of our disagreement for sure."

"When do you go?"

"Nick's gassing the van right now. We'll drive to LA and catch the redeye."

I shifted back and forth from one foot to another. I didn't want to be there when Nick returned, but wanted every minute I could have with her. "How long do you think you'll be gone?"

"Hard to say. Island time is different. I'm guessing a month, perhaps a week or two beyond that."

I dreaded the long, lonely stretch ahead. My world was changing fast, the ground disappearing into familiar insecurities.

"Please come here on the weekends. Enjoy the beautiful spring." She pointed to the ground. Early spring flowers, jonquils and tulips, bloomed in her front garden. "Nothing needs much care. Melting snow keeps the beds moist."

I hugged her.

"Relax. Bring a friend."

I couldn't tell her she was my only one. "It's all so sudden." I looked at my feet, trying not to cry.

"Life's sudden." Smoothing the hair from my forehead, Pia kissed my cheek. "Aloha, Laura." She went inside for her bag.

I walked up the hill and out to the highway.

Although I feared life without Pia would be dull, my spring semester classes proved both challenging and engaging. Her absence made me pay more attention to my peers. Bar owners in the small college town often ignored legal drinking age, serving minors when an older student ordered, looking the other way when the pitcher was shared. Wednesday nights, many students sought a mid-week break from studies and local taverns cashed in. One evening I tagged along with my housemates. No longer used to whiskey sours made with sugary mix and cheap booze, spoiled by Pia's elegant concoctions, I paid the price of my indulgence with a killer hangover the next morning.

I missed classes and limped to the drugstore, my headache demanding a slow pace. That's the first time I saw him. Regardless of Pia's advice to focus on character, I noticed his height, several inches over six feet. His light brown hair, parted on the side, had a natural wave in front, and brushed his collar in back. Longish, but neat. Worrying that I must look as bad as I felt made me keep my head down and tip-toe toward the pain relievers.

"Alka-Seltzer Plus?" The gentle giant magically appeared in the same aisle.

Concerned about vomiting all over him, I didn't risk opening my mouth, but nodded.

"I always recommend a good run. Once you get over the queasiness, your head stops pounding." He walked behind me to the checkout counter.

Dismayed my condition was so obvious, I muttered "Thank you" and paid the clerk.

My one-man fan club followed me out the door and along the sidewalk. "Nice day." His legs were so long that for each step he took, I needed three. And I couldn't move fast. Sunglasses covered my puffy, bloodshot eyes. I got away with another nod.

"Meet me at the Quad in twenty and we'll jog around the grass," he said.

The idea of jogging nauseated me all over again, but I wanted desperately to see him. "Okay," I croaked. Back at the dorm, I drank the Alka Seltzer, splashed ice-cold water on my face, and laced up my running shoes. "You can do this," I told my reflection in the bathroom mirror.

I strolled slowly to the Quad. He showed up, a promising sign. I wanted a man who did what he said he would. "Sam." He offered his hand. I thought it a sweet, old-fashioned gesture. When he smiled, his dark blue eyes crinkled at the corners. "And you're Laura? I see you at language lab sometimes." He noticed me; he knew my name. Two gold stars. And he could run, too, on those beautiful, muscular legs. My slow pace allowed me to watch. Sam trotted around the perimeter of the Quad at least twice before I completed the square. He looked me up and down. "Not much of a runner, are you?" Another good sign: he spoke the truth. He took off again. "I need a shower," he said when he got back. "Want to grab a burger?"

"I'm never eating again." I groaned and pulled my shades from my eyes so he could assess the damage.

"Oh, yeah." He bent to examine my face. "Maybe we should postpone until this weekend." For a moment I thought he might kiss me. *Please, not now.* His breath smelled like cinnamon. Mine tasted sour. When I stepped back, he got the message.

We'd agreed on casual. I wore a lacy bra and my best underpants under a simple linen sheath. Even in heels I'd be shorter than he, and chose an unadorned pair. Sam was wearing a soft blue Oxford shirt, tail tucked into navy chinos. No tie, but a tan sports coat. Decent leather shoes. He picked me up on campus in an old Studebaker that had been his grandmother's car. Unfortunately for him, she hadn't been tall. He opened the door for me, another point for Sam, then squeezed his lanky frame into the driver's seat. Any fantasies I had about sex after dinner disappeared. We'd never achieve a prone, or even half-prone position in the tiny automobile.

The radio took the place of conversation as he drove through town, until I noticed we were driving across the Milton-Madison bridge. "Hey, I thought we were going to Sunny's." I named a café popular with college students.

"Yeah, I know that's what we said. But when I thought it through, I figured we'd see a bunch of people, and, you know…"

"What?" I didn't know.

He raised his eyebrows. "Privacy."

"Okay." I liked that he didn't want to share our time with others. "Where are we going, then?"

"Hill House."

"You're right. We won't run into anyone." Another plus for the Sam List: he cared enough to spend money on me.

No one at the upscale restaurant would serve us liquor, forcing us to engage in coherent conversation. No loosening of the tongue, no *in vino veritas*. We sounded exactly like who we were: two college students flirting, brushing our legs under the table, high on the chase, hopeful. By the end of the meal, after the appropriate exchange of pleasantries, I knew Sam came from a small town near Cincinnati, had three brothers, and studied history. He found out that my relatives lived in Cincy and that I'd declared an English major. During our dialogue I planned how to get him into bed. Discourse for the sake of intercourse.

The duration of our date proved physically painful. Part of me wanted our attraction to be intellectual, even spiritual, but it had more to do with carnal lust. When Sam didn't park for a make-out session on the way back to campus, I made my move. "Know the road off the highway past the main college entrance?"

"Yeah."

"Well, I happen to be taking care of a friend's place while she's gone. Would you drop me off there?"

The Studebaker made it down Pia's driveway. Sam walked me up to the porch.

"Come in while I light a fire in the woodstove. The spring nights are still chilly."

Taking a cue, Sam put his arm around me as I unlocked the door, both arms around me once we were inside. My body flushed, responding the way it hadn't with Pat, with plenty of heat. Taking one of Sam's hands in mine, and pulling him behind me, I switched off the porch light and turned on a floor lamp in the living room so we could see our way to Pia's bed. I turned my back; he unzipped my dress. We each removed our own clothing, taking care to fold and stack things neatly. Sam stopped to hang up his shirt in the closet. And grab condoms from his pants pocket. The lights stayed off.

We dove under the comforter. Skin to skin. Investigating, discovering, fumbling to find a good position, determined to complete the act. Soon we found a slow, steady rhythm. Sam waited for my climax, then began to thrust hard, deep, and fast until he reached his own. His loud groan made me glad we were in the middle of nowhere instead of a car or dorm room. After he rolled off, we lay side by side until our breathing evened. We kissed gently now and then. I wondered what to say.

Sam sat up in bed and leaned against the headboard. When I switched on the bedside lamp, a soft glow revealed our nakedness. We began to explore with both hands and eyes. Sam slipped an arm around my shoulders, nuzzled my neck and ear, stroked my breasts. All the while I made oohs and aahs of pleasure. He pulled back the comforter. Lying down, he placed his palms over my nipples. My breath quickened. Then, kissing and licking, his mouth toured my lower body. Eyes closed, I moaned. "Again?" I thought, but must have spoken aloud, because he nodded. Afterwards we drifted into sleep. Entwined, we fit perfectly.

Some minutes, or maybe hours later, Sam cradled my face in his hands and I opened my eyes. He whispered in my ear. "Your first time?"

"And second."

His eyes searched mine. "Me, too."

I didn't know if I believed him. He'd performed all the right moves, especially with the condoms. Fast, definite. I wondered if guys practiced ahead of time. Deciding not to push the subject, I kissed him.

I woke first, desperate to pee and brush my teeth, and shivered my way to the bathroom. Pia's bathrobe and pair of slippers seemed to fit me well enough, but I checked my reflection in the full length mirror, hoping not to look clownish. I also wanted to see if losing my virginity had made me look sophisticated. It hadn't.

Closing the bedroom door, careful not to make noise, I started a fire. The kindling caught split pine right away, and, within minutes, delicious heat warmed the air. Searching the fridge for food suitable for a lovers' breakfast, I regretted my spontaneity. I hadn't shopped. All I could offer Sam would be toast from a loaf in the freezer. The jar of apple butter, a ring of rust around its rim, passed a smell test. Coffee would be served without cream. Sam's question, "Your first time?" boomed in my head. Had my inexperience been obvious? Had I done something weird?

I didn't hear him behind me, and jumped when his arms encircled my waist. "You're a trusting soul." He turned me around to face him. "Inviting me in like that." Sam hadn't dressed. He untied my sash, and lifted the robe away from my shoulders. "Let me get a good look at you, girl."

Wishing to say something clever, I let my eyes travel up and down his body. Desire made words impossible. My mind saw us having sex in the kitchen. Pondering creative positions,

I decided it was too soon. Sam might think I was some kind of nymphomaniac. I forced myself out of my reverie and back into the robe. "Breakfast?"

"Sure." Sam sat on a stool at the counter. Making no move to get his clothes, he watched me grind coffee beans. "Nice place."

"Yeah." I pushed the toaster handle and waited for questions. Respecting Pia's privacy seemed important. Then again, she'd said to bring a friend, implying a friend like Sam would be welcome.

"Who lives here?"

"A woman named Pia." I reached into the cupboard for mugs and wondered how much to volunteer. "She's an artist. After breakfast I'll show you the studio out back. The walls are painted to look like Hawaii, where she is right now."

"Okay. Cool. Know if she deals pot?"

"What?" Glad my back was to him, I smeared apple butter on the toast. "Of course not."

"Meaning you don't know, or, of course she doesn't?"

Placing our plates on the table, I poured coffee. "Come, eat." Maybe he'd drop the subject. "Sorry. Not much in the fridge. I'm only here on weekends."

He took a bite. "There's a campus rumor about a little house in the woods."

"Really?"

"Yeah." He sipped, then made a face. "Is there anything sweet?"

"Sorry." I scooted my chair back.

"Stop apologizing." Sam stood. "And sit down. Tell me where to look, and I'll get it myself."

"Third shelf up, on the right."

"Got it." He pulled drawers open until he found silverware and came back with a bag of sugar and two spoons. "Want some?"

"Sure. Thanks."

"I don't drink coffee much. More of a juice guy."

'Sorry' sprung to my lips, but I brought a napkin to my mouth, and Sam didn't hear me.

"One story says a pretty lady who lives in a house near the river likes to get stoned and do favors for studs brave enough to make it down Devil's Backbone."

My laugh caused me to spew a little coffee onto my chin. "Sounds like a fairy tale guys would tell."

"Yeah, guess you're right." He shrugged. "Another version says a guy in a wheelchair likes to watch."

I laughed again, amused how bits and pieces of truth had become exaggerated and mismanaged. "Her husband, who died a year ago, used a wheelchair." Looking down into my lap, I made my voice extra sad.

"Oh." Sam's face turned red. "Sorry." He reached for one of my hands. "I didn't mean to be disrespectful."

"Don't apologize." I lifted my face and smiled. "Let's talk about something else."

"Okay." He took a bite of toast and wrinkled his nose. "How about going to the Cabin for breakfast?"

On Saturday mornings the Campus Cabin, a mom-and-pop greasy spoon on the edge of campus, served one purpose.

Couples who'd had sex the night before showed up and showed off. The gesture didn't imply commitment. One-night stands joined long time steadies in a parade that fueled gossip all week long. Singles sat at the counter to ogle the couples in the booths. The frat guys had crude names for each day of the week, Make-Out Monday to Slutty Saturday. It wasn't hard to guess what the F in Friday stood for. Part of me resented Sam for asking, another part would be proud to join the club. Stalling for time, I removed our plates from the table and scraped the toast into the trash. "Let's go to Sunny's for cinnamon rolls." I watched his face for disappointment. Saw none.

"Good idea." He left the kitchen in search of his clothes.

This time last year, Pat's lack of passion had made me doubt my sex appeal. During my sophomore spring, I gave my body to Sam. We met between classes, and kissed behind the admin building. Weeknight study dates meant spreading a blanket in the yard of his fraternity house and petting to the brink. We deserved the PDA trophy his brothers presented to us as a joke. "No kidding, Laura," one of my roommates said. "No one can talk to you these days 'cause your tongue's always in Sam's mouth." Oblivious to peer criticism, I shrugged off the comments and teasing.

Each weekend, after a grocery store run, Sam and I headed for Pia's. We loved playing house. I cooked his favorite meals: simple tuna casseroles and an easy chicken-cornflake dish, mushroom soup-goop. We drank Pia's wine. Although he wasn't musically talented, Sam could carry a tune and didn't mind singing along or dancing with me to Pia's outdated records. My favorite was Ella Fitzgerald singing Cole Porter's *Let's Do It*. "Birds do it, bees do it, even educated fleas do it." I would wait, hoping Sam would pick up the chorus, "Let's fall in love."

When the weather got warmer, we walked around without clothes. More comfortable in my skin, I became proud of my breasts, which I'd always thought too small. Sam said he admired every inch. I grew more adventurous in bed. Our original union paled in comparison to new pleasures, positions never tried, or imagined. I discovered I'd never had a real orgasm when my first one took me to surrender.

With access to Pia's house, Sam and I had a different kind of time than most college students, who lived and partied in groups. Our frequent sexual couplings were punctuated with conversation. We exchanged childhood stories and campus gossip, compared profs and courses. At first, every word he said was magic, but, by the end of the third weekend, I wished Sam's body had Pat's mind. I wanted to discuss Life. With Pia, I'd grown used to talking about art and spirit. To his credit, Sam listened well, but he lacked responses to my deeper questions, and I soon tired of my own chatter. One evening I made a proposal: "Let's do something different."

"Whatever you want." Sam kept kissing his way up my arm.

"An art project."

He stopped and laughed. "My greatest masterpiece comes from fourth grade. Mother's Day. We glued fake seashells on terra cotta flower pots. I'm afraid that was my last, and final, attempt at art." Head dipped, he mimicked Elvis. "Thank you very much."

"Come on." I had promised to show him Pia's studio, but we'd been too busy in the house.

"Ahh, this is cool." Sam ran his hand along the edge of a cresting wave. He touched the tops of palm trees.

"A game, then?" I opened the craft cupboard. "Choose three things."

"In second grade I spelled my name with macaroni." He grabbed something from the top shelf. "I also remember making potholders and lanyards at summer camp. Close your eyes." Making a great show of hiding materials under his shirt, Sam shuffled toward the work table.

"Don't you peek." I made my choices quickly. "Stay on that side of the room. You've got half an hour. Go!"

"Hold on. Is this a race or a competition?"

"Hush. I don't know. Just start."

"How about some glue?"

I tossed him a bottle of Elmer's.

Each of us worked in silence for about thirty minutes, timed by a clock on the dresser. The face didn't glow in the dark, and the sun was setting. The spring evening grew cool, so we straightened up, then took our finished pieces back to the house. Sam lit the woodstove while I made soup. After we ate I said, "You first."

"No fair." But he held up his creation, a mask. "Ta-da!" When he placed it over his face with a flourish, the transformation startled me. With the sides of his eyes covered, he looked older. The black velvet fabric he'd used for the basic mask highlighted his fair skin. The turquoise feathers glued around the dark edges made me think of a lanky bird.

"Let me guess." I wanted to keep the game going. "Lone Ranger? Show girl?"

"No." Sam removed the mask with both hands and stared at his creation.

Sure that he was about to reveal its symbolism, I didn't speak.

He shrugged. "I really don't know why I came up with this."

"Don't be embarrassed. Keep it on."

"What did you get into?" Sam pushed his mask to the side of his plate.

Extending my arm, which I'd been hiding under the table, I revealed a colorful bracelet. Tiny beads on a thin wire snaked from wrist to elbow. When I twirled my arm, the beads caught the lamplight.

"Like a kaleidoscope." Sam's deep voice made me want to kiss him. I moved to his lap. He wrapped me in his long arms, and the evening, like every other, ended with sex.

One Saturday morning we lingered in bed. "Let's have some people over." Sam tried to make the suggestion sound spontaneous, but I could tell he'd rehearsed.

"Like who?"

"Maybe Gary and Lisa, or Jim and Polly?"

Sam's fraternity brothers. I knew them slightly. The girls belonged to the sorority best known for drinking. "Not a good idea. This place belongs to someone else. I'm worried about it getting trashed, actually I'm worried about telling anyone else how to get here. Pia trusts me to protect her privacy." I'd rehearsed my speech as well.

"Come on. The guys are solid." Sam's fist tapped his open palm in some kind of secret frat sign. The gesture failed to reassure me. "We'll have an early night."

"It just doesn't feel right." I tried to sound casual without insulting his friends. This was the closest we'd come to a disagreement.

"Okay, no problem. In that case I'll hang with the bros next Saturday."

"That's fine." I tried not to feel punished.

S am spent the next weekend on campus, and I was alone when Pia returned. Someone must have dropped her off at the top of the hill, because I didn't hear her coming. I was kneeling in the front flower garden, picking pansies and tiny daffodils. She saw me from the back, like the first time we met, "Aloha, *wahine*. Who is he?"

For a moment I wondered how she knew, but didn't ask. Instead, I turned around and stepped into her open arms. "Sam, my Sam. You're going to love him. He's everything I asked for."

"The ancestors listen. And they also talk. I spent the last month listening to one." She rolled her eyes. "For hours at a time." She put her suitcase down, looked at the budding trees, and took a deep breath. "Beautiful, so quiet."

Glad that neither Sam, nor his friends were here, I took her bag and carried it inside.

"You can meet him tonight. Unless you're too tired. or would rather be by yourself."

"What I need is a hot shower."

While she bathed, I placed spring flowers in vases and made her bed with fresh sheets. I hummed. My two favorite people in the whole world were about to meet. Hair still wet, Pia came out of the shower wearing something that looked like a bra on top with a matching flowered cloth tied around her hips. She noticed my stare. "Like it?" She twirled around and I could see how tan her legs were. "They're all the rage in

Hawaii. Some fashion genius got the idea that the top of a two-piece bathing suit would look great with a sarong."

"Genius is right." I admired the drape of the fabric. "It's outrageously sexy. I certainly don't want Sam to see you in it."

"Laura, are you serious? You remind me of my father." Pia tried not to laugh. "And not in a good way."

"Sorry. That just popped out. But it's true. His first look at you will be his last at me."

"Give me some credit." Pia went to her bedroom and returned with another cloth and top. "This is yours. Try it on."

Hugging her, I said "thanks" into her hair and kissed her cheek. My new found sensuality made affection easy, a new language to share with Pia. "I'll change in the studio."

My ensemble blossomed blues and greens, perfect for my coloring. Posing in front of a three-way mirror, I delighted in my womanly self. Humming a ukulele tune, I started a fake hula dance. My hips and arms did not cooperate. Not even close. My little one-woman show was interrupted when I heard Pia arguing with someone, a man. I couldn't hear what they were saying, but the tones in their voices were certainly not friendly. The cadences of relaxed conversation were missing. Too many long pauses, followed by short bursts of sound. Oblivious to anyone but Sam, I'd forgotten about Kevin, Pia's college boy lover. And the trouble with her cousin Nick.

Hoping my presence might diffuse the situation, I made a great deal of noise as I came through the back door. Sure enough, the exchange quieted. "Hi." I extended a hand to the tall stranger. "I don't think we've met. I'm Laura."

"Benjamin Draper, glad to meet you." He looked surprised to see someone else, especially someone else dressed like Pia. "My sister Janet mentioned seeing you up on campus. Last winter." He had an odd way of making the statements sound like questions.

"That's right." I nodded, removing my hand from his grasp. *You're ten times more polite than she was.*

"I hear you'll be staying here awhile," he said.

News to me. I hadn't given much thought to what would happen when Pia returned from Hawaii. Sam and I had played house here every weekend, and sometimes on an occasional school night when papers weren't due. Moving back to campus would certainly limit our sexual freedom, maybe even end our relationship.

Pia caught my confused look. "That's right, Ben. Laura's moving into the studio."

"Now, Pia," Ben started gently, then his deep voice gained command of the room. "Mama and Pop have been more than generous. The agreement was that after a year you would move into the studio so they could rent out the house."

"Did I sign something?"

"The family discussed this before Charley died. It's not fair they have to keep paying the bank." Emotion started to get the best of him, his face grew red. "Hell, you were the one who suggested it."

"That's all it ever was, Ben, a suggestion. I'm not legally bound." Her voice, though firm, grew softer. "And it's not fair Charley died, either."

Ben had the sense to keep quiet.

Pia switched gears. "I returned from Hawaii this afternoon. You've caught me at a bad time. Laura and I are expecting visitors." Dressed in scant tops, breasts pushed up and out, bottoms swathed in flowery cloth, we must have made his day. I noticed he kept trying not to look. "We need to make dinner." She motioned me toward the kitchen.

Eyes to the ground, Benjamin Draper hesitated. "Okay. Get in touch with me after you're settled."

"Of course." Giving him an energetic wave, Pia beamed at him.

We waited until we heard his truck leave the driveway before we got the giggles. Not about the situation, but the picture Ben Draper made, country casual in jeans. Short-sleeved plaid shirt, tucked in. "The Glen Campbell type." I said. "Wonder what he thought."

"Oh, he'll go back and tell Mama and Pop a story that won't be to my advantage."

"Really, like what?"

"No doubt my morals will be questioned. He'll say I'm not being faithful to Charley's memory. They want a real widow, who wears dark colors and knits. Pia opened the refrigerator. "What a mess."

"I cleaned." I said, thinking she was talking about the food.

"Tutu warned me." Handing me the contents of the vegetable drawer, she reached for a long chopping knife. "I didn't expect him quite so soon. Seems I've sold myself down the river again. All for a man."

"What do you mean?"

She chopped potatoes with more force than necessary. "Disobedient daughter," – chop – "loving wife," – chop – "family tattle-tale," – chop – "ungrateful daughter-in-law." Silence. "Please put a pot of water on to boil."

"Okay." I poured two glasses from a bottle of champagne that had been waiting in the fridge for her homecoming. "Trade you." I took the knife and handed her a flute. Clinking mine to hers, I smiled. "*Á kàlè má luna*, Cheers!"

"Good. You learned something worthwhile from me." Pia's sarcasm soured the celebration.

"Jet lag?" I pulled a kitchen stool to the counter. "Sit. Tell me. I'll cook."

"The problem is that Tutu gives me too much information about myself." She took a sip. "She points out the choices I've made and shows me they've created the pattern of my life. *Ulana*." Pia set her glass on the counter and interlaced her fingers. "There's really no word for it in English. *Weaving* comes closest."

"Didn't you and Nick go there to help her?" I plopped the potatoes into the pot.

"Nick and I were summoned by our grandmother, reprimanded for our wrongdoings, and assigned our tasks. According to Tutu, the ancestors are demanding reparations."

"Which are?"

"Nick performed hard physical labor to atone for the use and sale of drugs. He built a stone wall around Tutu's backyard and ended up doing work for her neighbors as well. Each time he finished one project, Tutu would say, 'Nakoa, *Brave*, you must work until the people who have taken your medicine are no longer ill.' That's what she calls drugs, medicine." Pia drained her glass, and held it out for a refill. "Nick looks great, by the way, and stayed in Kauai. He claims he wants to keep an eye on Tutu, but I suspect it has more to do with his lovely new Hawaiian girlfriend, whom he met after we were there about five minutes."

"No surprise there." I chopped celery.

"'Pilialoha, *Beloved*,' Tutu said, 'you must honor your talent.' It took days for me to figure out she meant for me to pursue an art career."

"You're already well on your way down that path."

"All this to gain *hohoponopono*, reconciliation and forgiveness. 'Now the world will test you,' Tutu said. 'Hasn't it already?' I asked. 'My husband died, what more can the old gods request?' 'Plenty,' she said. 'Charley's life paid only a small portion of the debt incurred when your mother renounced her heritage.'" Pia held out her glass once more.

"She really takes the heritage stuff seriously." I put a plate in front of her. Apple, cheese, peanut butter.

"No kidding. Apparently my childlessness is a direct result of my mother's lack of *ho ihi*."

"Do you believe that?"

"I'm not sure, but I do believe Tutu saved our souls. Nicky belongs there. He needs to be held accountable." She picked up a slice of cheese and took a bite, then waved it in the air. "But, as I explained to my grandmother, I am a free, independent, and presently impoverished adult woman who must make my own way."

"You've done that." I dripped some olive oil over the warm potatoes.

"From where you sit, sure, I get how you can think so." She watched me add spices. "Tutu personifies matriarchy. Even though she married a *haole*, the blood of Papa and Wakea flow through the veins of her own children and into their souls. When my mother married a *haole*, it should have made little difference. But Tutu says Mom's conscious rejection of old Hawaii 'betrays all women who came before and damns all women who came after.'"

"Where's your mother now?" I offered Pia a taste of potato salad.

"I don't know, exactly." She licked the spoon." The last time I spoke with my parents was seven years ago, right after Charley's accident."

"And Tutu? Does she know?"

"If she does, she's not saying. When Charley died, I wrote a letter to the last address I had for them. No response. And the letter wasn't returned."

"Oh." I paused. "You must have felt so alone." I took a sip from my glass. "I would have."

"Charley's family offered their brand of support. Aunt Tina and Nick drove to the memorial, made leis and sang the death songs. I had a service here, at the house, because Charley built it and was happy here. Mostly."

Before she indulged in further sadness, I turned my attention back to dinner and looked at the clock. "It's nearly seven. Sam might show up tonight."

"Kevin's coming, too. He's hot to get me back in bed. What kind of sex do you have with Sam?"

A month ago the question would have caused me to blush. Now it made me glad to have Pia back, but I had no idea what she meant. "The normal kind?"

"Charley and I made lots of different kinds of love over the years."

I could tell she was about to impart an important lesson.

"Intimate sex is what every woman wants, but most men have two speeds, power drill or slow motor boat." Despite the snacks, Pia seemed a little drunk. "Make-up sex can be good. Sexual barter can be fun." She'd never been this flippant about Charley, ever. "You'll find out." She winked. "Come, help me set the table."

The evening grew cool, and Pia placed a shawl of filmy silk over my shoulders. Kevin and Sam arrived at the same time. We could hear them introduce themselves as they walked down the driveway. Sam, taller than Kevin by several inches, wore his standard olive-drab army jacket. Kevin, richer than Sam by God knows how much, wore a designer polo shirt and a light windbreaker. Sam's formerly baby-smooth upper lip now prickled with the beginnings of a dark mustache, but Kevin, lean and lithe, looked more like a man than Sam.

When he saw us in the glow of the porch light, Kevin put his hand on his heart. "Flowery clouds of beauty, exotic Sirens. Stay right there. I want to draw you both, just like that. You're a gorgeous vision of loveliness."

Sam rolled his eyes. I put a finger to my lips and shook my head.

"Not tonight." Pia opened her arms. She didn't even look at Sam. While Pia and Kevin continued to kiss, I took Sam's hand and led him to the kitchen. Quickly, silently, I prepared a tray. Heaps of potato salad, fresh watermelon slices, spicy deviled eggs. Sam always brought his appetite. "Pic-nic," I mouthed. Motioning for him to bring a bottle of red wine, I walked him out to the studio. "You can meet her in the morning."

"Okay." He unwound my shawl and gave me one long admiring gaze before reaching behind me to unhook the bra top, then he untied the sarong and let it fall to the floor. "I missed you."

Pia and Sam did not become friends. Once in a while Sam would pester me about the drug rumors. I dismissed the matter as myth, but feared if left alone with Pia, he might bring up the subject, and she would think I'd tattled. For the most part they danced around each other, vying for my time and attention. Between them my life stayed doubly busy and happy. Love struck, I'd neglected to register for a class needed for my major. If I wanted to graduate with my class, I would have to go to summer school. Dad refused to pay tuition. My accumulated savings, waitressing tips from three summers, added up to just enough to cover course costs. At the beginning of June, I moved from campus into Pia's studio.

College boys acted like bands of Indians roaming the Plains, seeking food and other comforts. My self-assigned task was to separate Sam from the herd and mark him as my territory. We'd been together a couple of months, and neither of us had said the L word. "You have a cold," I told Sam one weekend. "Miss the party. Stay with me." He was lying across the bed in the studio. "I'll nurse you back to health." My blouse came off. He stayed. Luring him with food and sex, I invented chores at Pia's and told Sam we were trading them for the studio's rent. We planted a vegetable garden, repainted her shutters, built a smooth stone path to the studio. Anything and everything was designed to keep Sam there. But, at semester's end, he headed home to Ohio to work weekdays in a pre-fab housing factory. Although he wasn't likely to meet any young women, other dangers loomed: nail guns, saws, wood dust. Every day we were apart, I said a prayer for his protection. If Pia was my Fairy Godmother, I was Sam's.

Weekdays became busy for Pia and me. I enrolled in two classes, the English Comp class I needed for my major and Children's Lit, for fun. During the summer, a local youth camp used the campus and hired Pia to teach drawing. Her students, most of whom worshipped her completely, ranged in age from five to fifteen. Illustrations, cartoons, sketches, and portraits papered the kitchen walls. Crayoned stick figures were displayed beside sophisticated charcoals full of light and shadow.

"We're going to run out of space." I shook my head.

Pia handed me more pictures and a roll of scotch tape. "Put these up in the hall, then." Her pay, from a grant, wasn't much, but she loved the kids, and the chance to explore her artistic talents.

Most weekends Sam drove to Kate Hall, while Kevin visited the front house. When our lovers weren't around, Pia and I took field trips, small day time excursions that involved a picnic and sightseeing. Neither of us had extra cash for gas. We didn't make it to Angel Mounds, nor did we visit the Drapers. They came to us. Unfortunately, we were home.

The Saturday morning before summer session ended, the first car came down the drive just before noon. Pia and I were shaking out a rug in the side yard. The occupants of the silver station wagon drove into a cloud of dust.

"Not exactly the way to receive company." Janet Draper Lowell exited the driver's seat. "And just fine for family."

I couldn't tell if she was joking. Probably not.

Pia let go of the rug and went to the passenger door. "Mama." She opened it and offered her arm to an elderly woman. "Lean on me." Mama pulled herself upright, and Pia guided her into the house. The rear passenger door opened. A tall gentleman emerged slowly, as if hatching from an egg. Well over six feet, he was no chick.

Janet said, "Come on, Pop. Inside. The heat's too much for you."

No one noticed me. Left outside, holding the corner of the half-clean rug, I was sweaty. And grouchy. No one had told me they were coming. The next car was a truck. Ben Draper got out, glanced at me for less than a moment, and went inside to join his family.

There was no shower in the studio, but I managed a quick sink-bath. My first impulse, mainly from shyness, was to leave Pia alone with them. My gut instinct told me she would want me there as soon as possible. I walked around the front, kept low, and got myself into a position to watch without being seen. The windows were open. I listened in.

"You are familiar with the term 'contract'?" Janet asked Pia.

"Now, Janet," Pop interrupted. "There's no call to be belittlin'. That's not what this is all about."

"Succinctly, then," Janet spoke in her professor voice, "you agreed that after our brother," she made a motion that included herself and Ben, "and their son," she gestured toward Mama and Pop Draper, "passed away, you would vacate this house and move out back to the little place he built for you."

"Charley Draper, my husband," Pia's normal lilt grew hard, "intended for me to remain here. The 'little place' is an art studio, or a rental, as I see fit."

"The papers?" Looking triumphant, Janet turned to her brother.

Ben produced a manila envelope he'd been holding behind his back and cleared his throat. "Um, we got these drawn up at the Evansville Bank last week." He handed the envelope to Pia.

"What have you all been up to now?" She sounded more curious than upset.

Time to make my entrance. "Hi, everyone!" I went in a circle, shaking hands. "Mr. Draper, Mrs. Draper, so glad to meet you. I'm Laura McKenna. I live out back."

"Laura's my tenant. She's signed a lease for next year, as a matter of fact," Pia announced.

I hadn't, but nodded, and beamed at the assembly.

"So, you see," Pia looked at each one of them and handed the unopened packet back to Ben, "all is in compliance with Charley's will."

"Perhaps your husband neglected to mention that he took a loan from Pop to finish this place." Janet's voice was only a degree above condescending.

"But he didn't neglect to pay back that loan two years before he died." It was Pia's turn for triumph.

"That true, Pop?" Ben turned toward the old man.

"Yep. It is." He'd hesitated only a beat.

"Then, what's this about payments you and Mama should be receiving?" Ben looked at Janet.

"When I was going through the books, I noticed Dad never marked the balance as paid. Also, he didn't charge near enough interest."

"Maybe because Charley was his son." Pia enunciated each word, matching Janet's prissy tone.

"So. You sent me over here last spring, knowing these records didn't exactly exist?" Ben looked at his sister. The set of his jaw said this was not the first time Janet had duped him into acting as her emissary on a mission less than honest.

"It's good to see you," Pop suddenly blurted out. He gave Pia a wide smile.

"You, too." Pia stood and took both of his hands in hers. "Anyone for lemonade?"

Yeses all around gave me a chance to escape to the kitchen. I poured tall glasses, garnishing the drinks with fresh mint. Conversation came to a halt, and I turned on some music to fill the uncomfortable silence. Light classical blew through the room.

"Janet," Pia looked directly at her sister-in-law, "I don't know what your fight with me is. All I ask is for you to let it go, for the sake of Charley's memory." Her hands mimed picking something up and placing it gently to one side. The gesture earned the slightest nod from Janet. "And Mama, Pop, Ben," Pia continued, "I know I'm not who you would have chosen for Charley, but you must at least respect that he chose me for himself."

The Drapers had nothing to say to her honesty. Ben offered polite good-byes and drove away. Pia gathered the glasses. We walked Mama, Pop, and Janet out, and waved them away with promises to come visit. Pia stared after the cars for a moment before picking up a corner of the half-clean rug we left in the yard. "Grab the other side." Over the next half hour, we restored order in the house and didn't talk until Pia said, "Let's get out of here. Go to town and get a sandwich. My treat."

The early hour meant the diner was empty, and we could speak with relative privacy. As soon as the waitress put our plates on the table, Pia started talking. "Tutu told me this would happen. 'The old man will agree with you.'" She shook her head in disbelief. "'Stand firm and they won't see through you.'" Leaning back into the booth, she smiled. "Charley didn't pay back that loan."

"What do you mean?"

"He saved the money for me." Pia took a bite of her sandwich.

My brain took a minute to register the information. "You took a huge risk, Pia. I'm glad I didn't know."

"Forgive me for not telling you earlier. Thanks for playing along."

"I'm not entirely clueless. One look at your face told me what to do."

"Ah." She put her hands together and bowed her head slightly. "Bless you, child. You did as I wished."

"Don't I always?" I wondered if Tutu had put a spell on me, too.

Pia took a loud sip of her milkshake, then held my eyes with hers. "You've been a great friend, Laura."

Been?

"Charley invested Pop's loan. It's not a lot, but at least a start. Nick couldn't know. Now the Drapers are past considering. Everything came together while I was in Hawaii. Guess what's next."

I didn't have to guess. I knew. "You're going to art school."

"Right you are. First semester's paid for."

"Don't you feel the least little bit bad about keeping their money?" A knot was growing in my stomach, and I pushed my fries away. "Don't they count as elders, or ancestors?"

Pia shook her head. "Day after Labor Day I start at UC, Berkeley. I'm taking Nick's apartment."

I had lots more questions, but her face said subject closed. "Good." I tried to mean it. "Congratulations." California, a universe light years away. My heart was sinking.

"Let me ask you this," Pia started. "What else came together while I was in Hawaii?"

"Me and Sam," I said, ignoring her pun, using incorrect grammar on purpose.

"Take the house."

"Your house?"

"Move in. You and your Sam. Find out if you really are meant for each other."

"You must know." I watched her face. "Or Tutu does."

"Perhaps. But you have to find out for yourselves."

"Thank you." I held back tears. "I'll miss you."

"Oh, honey." Pia got up and came over to my side of the booth. She scooted close and draped her arm over my shoulder. "You have no idea."

She was right. I had no idea that Sam would say, "Yes, I'll come live with you," that Dad, thrilled to save college housing costs, would send spending money every month. I had no idea how much I feared getting pregnant. Some girls took the Pill, obtained for them by their married older sisters. Like booze, contraception for unmarried minors remained contraband. For several months, and while we lived apart, Sam didn't mind using condoms. Even though both of us wished for the feel of skin on skin, we never let that happen. In light of his powerful sex drive and my newly found ease with nudity, I kept condoms throughout the house and hid them before anybody dropped by.

Once word got out that Sam and I were shacking up, we were coerced into giving a housewarming party. As soon as his friends could find our new home, they visited often. Many evenings at dusk several guys would wander down the Backbone, six-packs in hand. Inevitably Sam would end up driving them back to school. I resented these intrusions into our pretend marital world, and let him know.

"Come on, Sweetie, it's no big deal." Sam defended himself by asking me questions: "What do you want me to say? That my friends aren't welcome here? You don't like them?"

"Of course not. Maybe you could give them a hint, though."

"Well, I don't exactly know how to do that."

I believed him. Sam was unfailingly polite. He opened doors for me. Most of the time he stood when I entered a room. He'd seat me at the table, even when we ate meals by ourselves. Mom would say he'd been "raised right." But he went brain-dead around his fraternity brothers. Together they would make crass sexual jokes about boobs and asses. "Jeez, Laura," Sam protested when I complained. "It's just guys being guys."

"Sorry you're a guy, then, I guess. My Sam is smarter than that."

"Listen, I was shy all through school, and never got picked for teams. I didn't ask girls out. We lived on a farm. For friends, I had my younger brothers, and one pal from eighth grade. When I got to Hanover, I vowed to make a fresh start. I played football my freshman year." He laughed. "God, I was awful, but did it anyway. Second semester I pledged Sigma Chi. You have friends for life after you go through that together." He hugged me. "I know we're crude. I'm sorry it offends you." Considering this was the longest speech he'd ever made, I was ready to drop the subject, but he continued. "Girl talk can get gross, too, I'm told."

"By whom?"

"Gus has a sister. Says they talk about wieners all the time."

"What is she, fourteen?" I made a superior, huffing noise. "We older women say dicks."

"See?"

"I'm joking!"

"Oh," he said. "We can't change the world, darling. I'll insist they whisper, okay?"

"Why do you ask me a question when you're telling me something, Sam?"

"Because I just don't want to talk about it anymore. There's no point."

"This is always where we end up."

"I know, honey." He hugged me close again. "I know." He patted my back as if I were a small child.

After these outbursts, Sam placated me by sticking around. Instead of going to weekend parties at the frat house, he studied with me. Jan and Doug, a couple we clicked with, came for dinner on Sunday nights. "You have such a darling place," Jan said. "So artsy."

"Thanks." I didn't bother to explain.

"Who did all these drawings?" she asked as she helped wash dishes.

This was a tougher question. One I sloughed off again. "The lady who used to live here," was all I said.

"She's talented. I see why you kept them up. Lends kind of a folksy feel, doesn't it?"

Artsy? Folksy? I wondered what Pia would think. Jan's question didn't need an answer, and I changed the subject to some banal chatter about a movie. Life without Pia wasn't as colorful, energetic, or intelligent. We'd been friends for less than a year, yet she'd become my mentor, sex educator, spiritual advisor, fashion consultant. I'd taken on new roles, too, her confidant, playmate, companion. Lying next to Sam, I missed Pia.

She planned to return for Thanksgiving. Excited to cook for her, I began researching recipes. Then she called to say that Nick would be visiting the Bay area, with his new wife, Hiwalani. "I can't wait to see them. She's pregnant!" Pia raved on the phone. "Tutu's proud to be a great grandmother, beside herself that Nicky married an Islander. They're going to live on Kauai."

"That's great." I tried to keep my voice even. "Think you'll get home for Christmas?"

"Maybe." Pia paused. "Did I tell you I made Dean's List?" She didn't ask about me, or Sam, or her beautiful little house near the river.

Thanksgiving turned out to be almost morbid. For the second year in a row, I told my folks I was going to a friend's; Sam told his family a similar tale. We set the table with Pia's good plates and goblets and invited other orphans to hodgepodge pot luck. "Careful of the tablecloth." I handed Sam a bottle of red wine.

"Why don't we stick with beer?"

"Not for special occasions." We ate typical college-student fare: mac and cheese, breadsticks dipped in tomato sauce, frozen pumpkin pie, the opposite of last year's feast with Pia. At the end of the meal, Jan stood and tapped her glass. "It happens Monday. Everybody come watch."

"What does?" Sam asked.

"Where have you been?" Doug looked surprised. "Oh, never mind," he added, glancing down the table at me. "Busy."

Sam grinned; I blushed.

The U.S. Selective Service System had announced a draft lottery for men born between 1944 and 1950. Before this, the Vietnam War meant little to me personally. Politics never captured my attention, but if Sam got called up, I planned to protest. On December 1, CBS would broadcast the draw.

Nearly fifty Sigma Chi members and those who loved them gathered around the TV in the downstairs rec room of the frat house. Order of call would be determined by birth date. We watched a Congressman reach into a deep glass jar atop a library stool. September 14. No one in the room was born on that day. Victory cheers followed. The guys began to chant: "No bros have to go!" On television, youth representatives continued to select birth dates, written on pieces of paper. These were handed to Draft Board officials, who pinned them on a big board with slots for each day, 366 to include Leap Years. The first boos came when Glenn, a senior, born September 7, 1948, posted at number 8. Everyone in the room realized he would most likely be called.

From then on a respectful silence remained throughout the game of chance. Perry placed fourteenth on the list. Joey eighty-seventh. Brad's birthday came in at 117. Sam's, 276. After that, I stopped paying attention. I'd been grabbing his hand so tightly that my whole arm tingled. I allowed myself a beer. I ate, finally, after what felt like a two day fast. Pizza proved a bad choice. "Take me home, Sam," I begged.

"Shh." He turned his attention back to the television. "It's still going on."

"Don't care," I whispered. "Feel sick."

"Twenty minutes, then we'll go." Sam could easily ignore me when the brothers were involved.

"All the guys at school are 2-S," he told me on the way home. "Making grades is critical."

Within a week, the threat of being drafted transformed Pia's from party house to study house. The guys arrived each night after dinner carrying text books instead of beer. We bought a tall bookshelf at the thrift shop and pushed it against the living room wall. Binders and slide rules took the place of poker chips and cards. I worried briefly that Pia might object to rearranging her furniture, but knew she would support our goal.

Sam read history texts aloud. I corrected spelling and grammar. Doug, a math major, and Jan, a psych student, filled out our valiant tutoring team. All the guys who studied with us passed finals. His social needs satisfied, Sam became dedicated. "Staying out of the war is the war. We don't need to march." My complaints about his lack of focus vanished. We didn't have children, but we were a couple with a mission, a cause.

Winter Break came with no word from Pia. Wanting Sam with me, I made plans for Louisville.

Sam declined the invitation. "Christmas is family time on the farm."

"At our house, too, in our own crazy way. Aren't you the least little bit curious?"

"Of course. I'll drive down the week after, okay?"

"Meaning we'll spend Christmas at your place?"

"I haven't exactly told my parents we're living together."

"That's okay. They do know about me, though? That you have a girlfriend?"

"We don't talk about personal issues."

"How about facts?"

"I was planning to tell them over break." Sam sounded defensive.

"So, we'll be apart for a week?"

"Sure. It might be good for us."

Exchanging gifts during a pre-Christmas holiday dinner, Sam handed me a small box. *Ring? He's taking me to his folks after all. Mom, Dad, meet Laura, my fiancée.* Inside the box a bracelet with a tiny gold chain held a few delicate stones. He'd chosen well. "Thanks, Sam." I held out my arm, and he fastened the clasp. My gift to him was utilitarian, a fairly extensive tool kit, something that would last. Examining each tool, he joked around. First he used a small wrench to adjust my ears, then placed the level on top of my head. He planted light goodbye kisses on my eyes and cheeks. When he drove away, the frivolity ended. Louisville without Sam would be dreadful.

On Christmas Eve day my sister called and asked for directions. Reluctantly, I told her how to find me. As I hugged the young woman who came to fetch me and take me to our parents, my heart longed for my little sister. "You've changed," I told her.

"You, too."

"How's school?"

"I quit. Didn't Mom tell you?"

I shook my head. Beyond a brief monthly phone check-in, I hadn't communicated with my parents for several months. "After one semester? What happened?"

"Robert." She smiled, her face looking like mine whenever I talked about Sam.

"But you've got your whole life ahead of you, Megs. You don't need to change it for a man." A part of me was giving myself the same advice.

"God, Laura, you sound like Mom." She gave her head an angry toss and frowned. "You're the one who's lived up to their dream." Slipping off her jacket, she followed me into the living room.

"What are you talking about?" I motioned her toward the couch.

"Your grades, the whole church thing."

I laughed. "All of that was to get out of the house."

"Robert's my way out." She smiled again. "I kind of half way live at his place already. "He's older. Twenty-six." She watched for my reaction.

Nearly a decade.

"Dad's threatening to have him arrested."

I kept my face in neutral, said, "Oh," took a deep breath and asked, "What does he do?"

"He's a second grade teacher at St. Matthew's."

"Are you getting married?" I couldn't help myself.

"Someday." She shrugged.

I wanted to ask her about the rest of her life, but didn't think the question fair since I hadn't a clue where mine was going. "Come see the rest of the house." I stood.

Meg oohed and aahed as we went from room to room. "How did you manage to swing this?"

"A friend lives here, and she's away at school."

"Must be a pretty good friend. Who did all these drawings, anyway?"

"Her kids." The look on her face made me add, "Art Camp students."

"Ready to go?" Her eyes searched for a suitcase.

"Never, really, for holidays at home."

Meg looked down. "Things are rough again."

"What's going on?"

"Dad's talking more shock treatments."

"Oh my God, Meg, why didn't you call me?"

"What could either of us do? He'll batter Mom with words until she commits herself."

"She must be complaining about his drinking again."

"Dad claims shock therapy makes her less argumentative. And that's true. Afterwards she's not upset about much at all."

"Meg, do you remember what Mom was like before her first stay in the hospital?"

"Not really. You took care of me more than she did."

"She's always cooperated with Dad, been more wife to him than mother to us. And this is how he repays her? Forces her to have her brain fried?"

Meg shifted her eyes to my tiny duffel bag. "How long are you staying?" She picked it up. "Doesn't feel like much in here."

"Right now I don't think I can last a minute." I moved closer to my sister. "Remember this?"

My eyes opened wide and both hands went over my mouth, a signal we had invented as kids. She'd been in second grade, I in fourth. We'd been tucked into beds in our shared room. Dad's rages woke us each night, and, without speaking, we'd leave our beds and sit, ears pressed to the door. The gesture started as a game. Our tongues hung out of silly faces, we bared our teeth at one another. But we also made a pact. We'd watch over Mom and never let on we'd heard them argue.

Now, Meg mimicked me before she spoke. "See everything, say nothing." We hugged. "You're welcome at Robert's. I already asked."

"Is he coming to Christmas dinner?"

"Yes."

"Thank God it won't be just us."

"He'll drink bourbon with Daddy and help Mom snap green beans. He'll sing a carol or two and play the piano."

"Happy for you, Megs." I kissed her cheek.

Christmas Eve I went to the midnight service at St. Paul's Episcopal Church with my mother. She didn't have much to say, but I could tell she was happy to have me there. And proud. We watched The Nativity Tableau performed by Sunday School students. A few years earlier, I had played the Glory Angel, the one who stands on a ladder over the Holy Family and shines the light onto the Light of the World. When the three Kings of the Orient came, bearing gifts from afar, singing as they walked down the aisle toward the manger, I squeezed Mom's hand. For a brief moment, I felt our connection.

Robert did indeed keep Christmas dinner from being the usual disastrous or boring event. He told funny stories about his grade school students. The day passed pleasantly enough, and I decided to spend the night. Lying in my childhood bed, a twin with a saggy mattress, alone in the room I'd shared with my sister, I took deep breaths. The Christmas service made me think about how long it had been since I'd prayed. My mother opened the door a crack. "Good night, Sugar."

The use of her endearment brought tears. "You, too, Mom, love you." My voice caught.

She came into the room and sat on the edge of the bed. "I miss you, honey." She stroked my hair.

"Mom, do you remember the year I played the Glory Angel?"

She nodded.

On the verge of telling her about Sam, that, like Meg and Robert, we were living together, I paused. "There are things you don't know about me."

Her face fell for a moment. "Let's not think about that, especially on Christmas." Her slow, southern voice comforted me. Managing to replace her concern with a soft smile, she bent close to kiss my hairline. "You'll have your own children."

The words sounded like both blessing and curse. Despite my precautions to ensure I wouldn't have kids, I did want them someday. I didn't want to be like Pia, who longed for children with her true love, and had been denied that opportunity. In my childhood bed, a prayer rose from my heart: *Help me respect my ancestors, may I not be childless.*

The next morning Mom left for church. Dad went to work. Their routine no longer included me. A part of me still longed for an alternate childhood, one in which I could be a daddy's girl or my mother's best friend. By lunchtime I was back in Indiana.

Pia arrived mysteriously that evening, populating the tiny island of my loneliness with her energetic world. After tea, I tended the fire and scooted the soft chairs together so that our knees touched. "Look, Laura." Pia turned a page of her sketchbook. "I'm working in pastels. Finally, my true medium." Each page of the portfolio revealed a simple wonder. Fruit or flowers, subjects for beginning artists, revealed subtle, unusual hues. A peach bore a light blue edge. Instead of traditional landscapes, Pia's hand rendered such a gentle effortless moonrise that the viewer felt released from gravity. One soft star glittered slightly. "Neverland," I told her. "Last star on the right, and straight on 'til morning."

"Exactly," Pia said. "I knew you'd see that." Her sense of color elevated the creations to master status and her drawings spoke a language anyone could recognize. Like Shakespeare, Pia was a humanist. Each composition evoked an emotional response. One portrait in particular, of a young Hawaiian girl, completely stole my heart. "Is that you?"

"Yes. It's from an old photograph I found at Tutu's. Me at nine. My island traits faded as I grew older. This girl, practicing hula in Tutu's garden, is pure Polynesian."

"God, it's fantastic!"

"My teacher thinks so. A few of my pastels will be featured in the Spring Show."

I leaned over and traced the young girl's cheek with my finger. "Quite an achievement for someone who promised to come home after one semester."

She sighed at my sarcasm. "Please be happy for me."

"I'm trying."

"Come to the opening in early March. I'll buy your ticket."

"I'd love to, but can you afford it?"

Pia ignored the question.

We spent the week catching up on news. She spoke about her teachers and classmates, by turns brilliant, funny, and awful. Berkeley was foggy, odd, full of hippies. "There's so much pot you can smell it when you walk down the street."

"That sounds weird."

"How's Sam?" She looked around for an indication that we were still living together. Her eyes rested on a pair of his shoes. "Where's Sam?"

"In Ohio. At his family farm."

"How come?"

"We decided to spend Christmas with our families this year."

"You mean he decided?"

"Right." Ready to confide in her, I sighed. "The longer we're together, the more confused I am about love."

"Love confuses everybody."

"That's what you said about sex."

"Remember all those talks we had about chemistry? For about six months Charley and I were one big exploding lab experiment. Then, when the reactions fizzled from time to time, we had to explore other subjects."

"Our lab's still blasting." I smiled.

"Something's different, though. I can feel it."

"Sam doesn't seem to have much drive, other than sex."

"Meaning he's a typical male college student?"

"I guess so. All through December we tutored guys from his fraternity who needed to make grades to avoid the draft." I pointed to the bookshelf.

"That sounds like a noble project."

I nodded. "One that lasted for all of three weeks. He doesn't think about the future."

"His own, or yours together?"

"Both."

"How about you?"

"My plans include a career."

"And a husband?"

"I always thought so."

"Sam's in the running?"

I shrugged. "The prime candidate."

"You need a bit more enthusiasm to convince me."

"I'm waiting."

"For what?"

"For him to say he loves me."

"And that means you'll love him back?"

"I already love the man he'll become." Even to my own ears, this sounded like something out of a schmaltzy love song. We both laughed.

"Good luck," Pia said. "I'd like to get to know Sam better. Last fall I was preoccupied with getting into school and didn't give him the attention he deserved."

"He gets plenty of attention from me."

"How's Kevin?"

"Great. He's at the Rhode Island School of Design. 'Pursuing his talent despite family disapproval.'"

"And what's the status of your … relationship?" I emphasized the last word.

"We've talked twice." She answered quickly. "We're on opposite coasts. I'm too old for him, anyway. Both of us knew that." She sounded like she was trying to convince herself.

"You've met someone."

"Who I'm sleeping with, you mean?"

"Yeah."

"Not yet. A couple of guys are interested." Pia smiled. "I'm older than most of the other students. Profs, though, and teaching assistants are good prospects."

"Meaning you will, soon?"

"Art's a sexy subject."

"Sexier than Shakespeare, that's for sure."

"There were some awfully saucy wenches in those plays, as I recall."

God, it was great to have her back. A little past midnight, Pia stood. "Don't move your things one bit." She slipped on a jacket and gloves, picked up her suitcase, and announced she would sleep in the studio during her visit. "I forgot how sweet that space is, and, besides, my art cupboard needs attention."

The next morning, she came into the house early and had breakfast ready by the time I got up. When she saw Sam walking down the driveway, she opened the door.

"Oh, wow." He stayed outside on the step. "You're back."

"Come on in. It's your house, too." Pia reached for his hand and pulled, gently guiding him into the living room.

Sam looked toward me. "Hi, hon." I walked into his arms. In front of Pia, he was awkward. His kiss landed on my eyebrow.

"How was Christmas?" I really wanted to know if he had missed me.

"Like Christmas. Too much food, too many gifts."

"Coffee?" Pia asked.

"Yes," Sam and I said at the same time. When she left the room, we kissed. Relieved that the fire still burned, I relaxed. "Now you two can get to know each other better." I held onto his arm.

Pia brought out a pretty tray with three mugs. "Let's sit by the fire. How are the roads, Sam?"

"A little wet." He added sugar to his coffee and stirred. "It's not cold enough to snow."

"When does school start again?" Pia knew the answer, but she was opening him smoothly.

"Wednesday."

The small talk continued until I couldn't take it anymore. "Sam, tell Pia about your junior trip to Gettysburg."

"Actually, it's Leesburg." He sat up straighter.

"Quite interesting, really," I added. "A small battle that turned out to be important. A Senator Baker got killed." Determined to elicit more than a few words at a time from Sam, I asked him a direct question: "Who fought there? Later became a Supreme Court Justice?"

"Oliver Wendell Holmes." Sam, off to a slow start, gained conversational momentum. "He served as a volunteer lieutenant." He looked at Pia's face to make sure she was interested.

Encouraged by her nod, he went on. "In 1861 he received a nearly fatal wound at Leesburg. He'll be the subject of my Independent Study next year."

"Every senior at Hanover College writes an undergraduate thesis," I explained.

"What's yours?" Pia asked me.

"Romantic Love in Shakespearean Tragedy."

Sam looked out the window.

"Perfect." Pia caught my eye and made a silent little kissing motion with her lips before turning toward Sam. "One of my American Art history texts has sketches by newspaper artists, guys who covered Civil War Battles. Would you like to see a few?"

"Sure, if it's not too much trouble."

"Stay right there. I'll get the book."

Two hours later, Pia and Sam were still discussing Civil War history, she, learning as much from him, as he from her. Their concentration meant there was no way I was going to get them into the kitchen. Back and forth with more coffee, then sweet rolls, I peeked in from time to time. "Look," Pia leaned over the book. When her dark hair fell into her face, she held it back with one hand, and traced the page with the other. "See the shadow on the belly of the fallen horse?"

"Yep."

"Right there." She tapped the page. "In the horse's belly, wet from the river, you can see the reflection of two dead soldiers."

"Oh, yeah." He turned the page sideways. "Their weapons must have been confiscated."

"I sure don't see any." Pia squinted into the drawing.

"Soldiers in a horse artillery brigade would have used both revolvers and sabers. Double deadly. I wonder what happened."

"We'll never know." My disinterest obvious, I began clearing the dishes. "Anyone like to take a walk?" I reached for my jacket. Sam stood and stretched his long legs.

"You two go on." Taking the plates from me, Pia headed toward the kitchen. "I'll make some lunch."

Late morning winter sun caught the edges of frost on bare trees. Sam took my hand. Careful not to be overheard, I waited until we were about a quarter mile from the house to speak. "What do you think?"

"That civilian war correspondents might make a better topic than Oliver Wendell Holmes."

"About Pia."

"Come here." He folded me into his arms. "She's cool." I waited. "But not as cool as you." His kisses made her disappear.

Over the next week, Sam, Pia, and I formed a tightly-knit triumvirate. My mother used to tell me not to put all my eggs in one basket. Carefully dividing mine in half, I found balance. A three-way division of labor meant that someone could always take a break. When Kevin arrived to visit for several days and made us four, we tag-teamed in the kitchen. Ladies cooked, the guys cleaned up.

Pia bought champagne for New Year's Eve, and we sipped in the kitchen. Kevin and Sam were playing five-card draw in the living room. We could hear their laughter. "Watch," she used a wooden spoon to stir a creamy sauce over low heat, "so you can make this for Sam when I'm gone."

"I don't want to think about that." My mother's words. "Especially tonight."

"We'll see each other in March." She added delicate flakes of parsley to the pot. "You'll love California."

Looking around her kitchen, inhaling the fragrant herbs, I wondered why she would leave again. "Right here, right now is perfect."

She turned from the stove to kiss me on the cheek. "Happy New Year."

At 10 pm we sang *Auld Lang Syne* a capella to welcome 1970. Kevin brought a painting he'd done in class, "from memory." Pia's likeness glowed from the canvas. His boast was well deserved, and his adoration struck me as sincere. The two artists retired to the studio, joking about posing nude for each other. In the bedroom, Sam handed me a circular disk that looked like a compact. "Open it. Let's start the new year right." A month's supply of birth control pills, one for each day of the week, sat happily in a perfect circle.

"How did you get them?"

"Larry Dean's older sister is trying to get pregnant."

"Are they safe?"

"I think so." He handed me a leaflet with instructions. "In two weeks."

"Do you have more?"

"Uh-huh." He dumped the contents of a paper grocery sack on the bed.

My eyes counted twelve disks. His smile, full of expectation, made me hope this was a sign of commitment, at least for a year. I asked for a glass of water.

In mid-January, Pia and Kevin returned to their schools, Sam and I resumed our studies. Academic pressure lessened at the beginning of the new term, and our tutoring sessions were put on hold. The party scene calmed down in winter. Alone, we began to bicker, mostly regarding household chores. When the time came to split and haul wood, Sam based his protest on a women's lib platform. I reminded him that the emphasis was on equality in the workplace.

"This is our workplace," he countered.

When our sparring made me cringe, I would give in. Gloves were needed to extract individual pieces of wood from the frozen pile. Hatchet in one hand, I'd use the other to pull with all my strength. I developed a method of using the tool like a crowbar to separate logs. Then, winded, angered by my body's weakness, I'd attack the firewood, pretending it was the head of a man. A war-mongering politician, an arrogant professor, my father. Never Sam. Regardless of who had wood duty, we managed to keep the fire going.

We were pinned, the college version of going steady. No one was quite sure of the meaning, other than outside parties understood we were unavailable. Sometimes Sam seemed uncomfortable with exclusivity. Naturally friendly, he flirted with other girls beyond the level of my comfort. Sam could sweet talk me into not minding so much, but I started holding little grudges, adding up the times he slighted me. On Valentine's Day he agreed to escort a frat brother's girlfriend to an event. "Jay's playing intramurals and Missy's Sweetheart Dance starts at 8. He's paying for my tux, her corsage, and dinner."

"Can't she skip it?"

"Oh, come on, Laura, they're seniors," he said, as if that should explain everything.

"Sam, don't say that."

"What?"

"Come on, Laura. Like it's up to me, anyway. You already said you'd go. Why pretend like you're asking me, or that you need my permission?"

"Well, I do care what you think. And I'd like your cooperation."

"You sound like my mom." It was all I could do not to roll my eyes.

He gave me a long delicious kiss. "Not your Mom."

I fretted away Cupid's holiday by baking heart shaped cookies. Belting back a few shots of Pia's best Scotch to invite sleep didn't work. Worrying, I watched the clock. A little past midnight, Sam stumbled toward our bed. "Move over, Baby." He sounded drunk.

"Take a shower first." I pushed him away, sat up and switched on the light. The minute I saw how gorgeous he looked in a tux, jealousy punched me in the gut. "Did you two make out?"

He wagged his index finger back and forth. "No, no, no, Mommy. Sammy good boy." Furious at his mocking, I kicked him in the stomach. He grabbed my foot. The rough and tumble went from serious to slapstick. We ended up rolling around on the floor in a wild tickle fight. "I love this!" Sam laughed. "I love you." The words slipped out easily, and my eyes asked him to say them again. He did, slowly, and with tenderness. Not exactly my original Valentine fantasy. No candlelit dinner or roses. Instead, a day late, and he'd gone on a date with another girl. But Sam said he loved me, and I vowed to love him back.

The last two weeks of February found me daydreaming through classes. Our declarations of love sparked fantasies of marriage. I filled the margins of my notebooks with script: *Mrs. Sam Jennings, Laura M. Jennings.*

Marie, one of my sorority sisters, was in the process of planning her summer wedding. A sophomore, she was marrying a senior, Dick, one of Sam's frat brothers. They planned to live off campus in a small apartment. While she finished at Hanover, he would commute to law school at the University of Louisville. I didn't know her well, but started asking lots of questions. Several dog-eared issues of bride magazines passed between us.

Whenever I suggested inviting them over for dinner, Sam always had an excuse. "What's with you?" I finally asked. "You usually jump at the chance to have one of your brothers here. Don't you like him?"

"Yeah. I do. But I don't get why he's letting her push him to the altar."

"They know they're right for each other. Why wait?" Hands on hips, I leaned forward to make my point. "Besides, he wants to get married as much as she does."

"Really?" He turned away, mumbling. "Not what I heard."

"Oh?"

Sam hesitated. "Go ahead. Ask them over."

Marie and Dick appreciated the invitation, but didn't commit. Proud of Sam for not betraying a confidence, I dropped the subject, but didn't let go of my wedding fantasy. One afternoon in Madison on errands, I walked Sam past the jeweler's window. "Look at the shape of this ring." I tapped the glass. He leaned over and squinted. From inside the salesman waved, beckoning us. I started for the door, but Sam shook his head, and I followed him down the street.

Flying west for Pia's art opening scared me. In my own social world, the age of twenty brought respect, but the rest of humanity would see me as a college student. An inexperienced traveler, I couldn't decide how or what to pack. Did the California weather demand shorts? I didn't have any. My dressy clothes for the opening made me look less than arty. What should I wear on the plane? The two times I'd flown with my family, Mom made matching dresses for Meg and me. The men on the plane would be wearing business clothes, the women would have jewelry. At the back of my closet I found a plain, navy blue skirt that descended slightly past my knees. I chose a blouse printed with tiny flowers, and a beige jacket. For shoes, low heels. The ensemble made me look like I might be heading for church.

Parting from Sam did not go well. His Studebaker barely made it to the airport in Indianapolis on time, and our good-byes were rushed. My rehearsed, loving wishes for him turned into last minute instructions. "Please keep the stove going. If it gets below forty-five degrees, the pipes will freeze. There's plenty of food in the fridge. Eggs, and milk." I couldn't think of much else to say. "And orange juice."

"Okay." While Sam hugged me, he kept looking over his shoulder at all the airport hustle and bustle. He didn't fly often either.

"That means don't get home too late if you go out." I wanted him to say he wasn't going out. "Are you listening?" My voice sounded shrill.

The gate attendant called passengers to board. "Bye." Sam kissed the top of my head. "Have fun!" He walked away from the gate. I waved at his back. "You, too!" Of course I hoped he wouldn't. The flight took most of the day. Too nervous to doze, too distracted to read, I spent air time looking at clouds out the plane window.

Pia didn't meet my plane. Instead, an Asian limousine driver navigated the freeways to Berkeley. Grey cement student housing towered over Nick's two story brick apartment building. "The place is safe." Pia had called the night before. "I'll leave a key for you under the mat. Get settled, or go explore. I've got class 'til six."

Inside, the walls bore square shadows from the buildings next door. Obviously, Pia had painted them. Instead of the tropical murals of the studio or the bright shades in her Indiana house, she used golden, rosy tones. The softness cradled me. Pia returned to find me stretched out across her bed. "You're really here!" She kissed my forehead. "How was the flight?"

"Bumpy." My hands dipped up and down. "God, I love this place."

"It's coming along." She sat beside me on the bed. Her eyes travelled around the room. "When I got here, the walls were a dirty white, offset by grayish yellow."

"Offensive to the core of your being."

"You know me well."

"How's the show coming?" I propped myself up on one elbow.

"Fantastic. The installation's complete, and the opening reception's tomorrow. We can walk over."

"Any chance we can eat before then?"

Pia laughed. "Get your lazy self up and we'll go for Chinese right this minute. Nick's kitchen's too small for real cooking."

King Yen's menu fascinated me. First, because most items were listed in Chinese characters and second, because the English descriptions still sounded foreign. Pia introduced me to eggrolls, duck, and prawns. Servers poured endless cups of green tea from flowered porcelain teapots. Atonal music piped through the busy restaurant, covering the clinking of dishes and buzz of conversation. By the time we left, a line of hungry would-be diners snaked around the corner.

"Ready to walk it off?" Ever the rebel, Pia suggested we try using her student ID to get us into the show a day early.

Berkeley's campus was only twice the size of Hanover's, but UC students outnumbered those of my college twenty to one. "Isn't it a rat-race?" I asked.

"Not at all. You've got to be pro-active, ask questions." She turned left toward a domed building. "If your focus is education, you need to schedule courses with profs instead of teaching assistants, of which there are many. Including *moi*."

"You're teaching already?"

"Beginning Drawing. And I do mean beginning. Some of the kids back at Art Camp could handle perspective better than my students."

"Still, that's got to be an honor, or a reward, or something. You haven't been here long."

"It's okay. They pay a small stipend." Pia brushed off my praise. "The class began in January." She stopped in front of a long building. "Here's the place. The gallery's on the second floor."

The main door opened with a gentle push. Inside, along a wide hallway, dark wooden doors bore brass name plates. "Faculty offices," Pia said. The freshly polished tile floor gleamed. Grander by far than anything at my school. "Listen." I whispered. The sound of machinery came from our right. Without talking, we walked down the hall to find a heavyset man, wearing headphones to block the sound of the cleaning equipment he operated.

"Let's see if we can get upstairs." Pia pointed to an open door behind the maintenance man.

I ducked under a velour rope, obviously meant as a barrier, and held it up for Pia. We took the stairs two at a time. "Turn left at the top," Pia instructed. The double doors to the gallery stood open. Venturing in, I stopped in the middle of the room to survey the collection. Each wall and partition, painted to highlight varying artistic styles, created a river of sensation. Pia walked in behind me, "I imagine it's like having several children. Which one gets the most attention?"

"The loudest." I approached a painting of a red amaryllis.

"Alan." Pia smiled. "You'll like him. He only paints red flowers. See what else of his you can find."

Although tempted to stop and admire her work, I wandered through the gallery to discover three more paintings by Alan. Next to a red sunflower I noticed a small gouache of tiny songbirds.

"Marilyn's," said Pia. "She's not nice."

"How can someone who paints cute little birds not be nice?"

"See for yourself tomorrow."

"Let's talk about yours."

"If we must."

"I'm pleased to see the face of the young *wahine* here."

"Yes, she made it past the jury."

"And, this one's your friend, Laura, right?" Pia's drawing showed me reading, head tipped forward into the book. My mouth formed a small round emphasis of concentration. The blue chair in her living room supported and uplifted me. She'd captured the serious student riding a cloud, unaware of her ethereal background.

"Are you angry?" Pia put a gentle hand on my upper arm. "I should have asked your permission."

"No ... flattered. You make me look like an angel without wings."

"Good."

"When did you do this?"

"Last summer. You were so used to me always having my sketch book, you didn't look up once."

"From pencil to pastel, then?"

"Yes. The colors fascinate me." Pia beckoned me toward another portrait she'd done. "Say hello to Matteo." Propped on one elbow, the man posed, lying across the bed in her apartment. He wore pajama bottoms.

"He's beautiful."

"Yes." She gazed admiringly at her own creation.

"Is he real?" I asked. "Sorry. Silly question."

"Art Practice Department Jr. Chair, UC Berkeley."

"You're his teaching assistant?"

"Yes. We started sleeping together about a month ago."

"Pia," I took her shoulders and turned her towards me, "tell me he's not married."

"Divorced. His ex-wife went back to Italy. No kids."

"How old is he?"

"Forty. But, don't worry, he hasn't lost any of his youthful enthusiasm."

Glancing at the painting of her handsome lover, I sighed. "Won't someone recognize him and cause a stink?"

"He looks different with his shirt on." She laughed. I don't think anybody could guess what's underneath." She ran her finger along the line of his well-built chest. "The tilt of his head is also uncharacteristic. He agreed to pose after several glasses of fine Italian wine."

"You were drunk-drawing?"

"Good one." She laughed. "I got the main sketch done before I felt a buzz. From the wine, that is."

"You bribed him." I pointed an accusatory finger toward her. "With more than booze."

The sound of floor polishing ended, and Pia put a hand on my arm, "We'd better scoot."

Back at the apartment, we sat at the table in the tiny kitchen. "How are things going with Sam?" Pia poured cups of mint tea.

"Okay, I guess. I still have to push him to make conversation."

"That will change as he gets older." She smiled. "For now, you've got me."

"Maybe we could join some service groups. You know, volunteer for a few good causes."

"Sign up yourself. Pick a project. He'll either help, or he won't." She shrugged.

"We've been together nearly a year," I leaned forward, "and he still hasn't told his parents about me."

"So that's what's really bothering you."

I nodded.

"Sam loves you." She took the last sip of tea. "Don't pressure him."

"But we're graduating next year. Then what?"

"Whatever you want. The next steps will become clear." Waving her hands in the air, Pia dismissed my concerns and yawned. "I'll be on the couch." She tucked me into her bed. "Sleep tight. Teo's taking us out for waffles in the morning."

I groaned. "What time?"

"Not 'til nine. Is that a problem?"

"Still full of Chinese." I patted my bloated belly.

"You're nervous about meeting him."

Was there anything she didn't know?

"Laura, Laura." Matteo took both my hands. "Let me look at you in person." He twirled me around gently, then kissed both my cheeks.

"Laura," Pia's voice came from behind us, "meet Dr. Corselli." He bowed his head toward me, and reached out an arm, scooping Pia close beside him. He wore a crisp ivory linen shirt and tailored slacks. Thick, wavy hair showed grey near his temples, laugh lines lived in the corners of near-black eyes. Together, they made a spectacular couple, as Pacific Island met Mediterranean. Back when Pia taught summer art camp, she'd blended crayons to match her skin: burnt sienna, gold, and goldenrod. Her lover's complexion shared the gold of hers, with olive added.

We ate waffles topped with fresh California fruit. Matteo asked me about both the college and Indiana. "Describe the climate." He urged conversation with a wave of his fork.

"Intellectual or social?"

"The weather." He chuckled.

"Oh. You've never been to the Midwest?"

"Only to the airport in St. Louis."

"Teo," Pia put a hand on his arm, "come see for yourself this summer."

He cradled her chin in one hand. "*Cara*, I'd really, really like to, but, as I have explained to you before, I must be 'writing to publish.' That is what professors are expected to do." Matteo's muscled chest puffed proudly. For the next twenty minutes, ignoring me altogether, stopping now and then to sprinkle Pia with endearments, *bella, stellina,* he expounded on his career plans. Perhaps his intention was to impress me. Maybe all European men acted like arrogant pocket dictionaries. I kept glancing toward Pia to see if she was having a similar reaction. She seemed entranced. When the waitress offered more coffee, I declined. The waffles became difficult to chew. Registering my distress, Pia rose from the table. "Please excuse us, Teo. Laura and I need to use the Ladies Room." She locked the door to the small bathroom. "What's wrong?"

"Does he ever talk about anything other than himself?"

"Of course." She didn't sound sure.

"How can you keep a straight face?" Kissing the air, I did my best imitation.

Someone knocked on the door. "Just a second." I turned on both faucets to cover our noise.

"Last night you said you wanted Sam to talk more."

"I meant have a conversation, not perform a one-man show."

"He's an artist. They're all like that."

"Defending him much?"

Another knock. Scowling at me, she whispered, "Point taken." She reached for the door latch.

I put a hand on her shoulder. "Order another cup of coffee. Let's stay and talk."

Pia nodded. We made our way back to our table, only to find it cleared and ready for the next diners. "*Piccola!*" Matteo waved, motioning us toward the exit. "Time to go. My day is busy. I'll see you at the reception." More cheek pecking for me, a full frontal embrace for Pia and a *"Ciao!"* loud enough for the entire restaurant ended the breakfast. Pia watched his back as he walked down the street. I started back into the restaurant, but this time her hand found my arm. "Enough. Let's play tourist."

We took the ferry from the Berkeley Pier across to San Francisco. The Golden Gate Bridge, high over the bay, busy with bikers and traffic, amazed us Ohio River girls. In the city, cable cars hurtled us up and down steep streets. At lunch time we ended up at Fisherman's Wharf. Even though still full from breakfast, we ate clam chowder from bread bowls. In China Town, Pia bought us two long silky scarves to wear on the way back across the water. We wrapped them, like turbans, to keep the wind from our hair. Back at the apartment we worked on makeup before getting dressed.

"Will this be okay?"

"Too plain," she said when she saw my long skirt and white blouse. Let's dress you up a little." From her closet she selected a gauzy cream colored blouse.

I shook my head. "My bra will show."

"So don't wear one."

"You've got to be kidding."

"I am, but you could get away with it in Berkeley." She laughed. "Free Love has done a lot for fashion." She brought out another top, a scoop neck, which worked well with the skirt. "You're lovely, Laura. You keep trying to hide. Show off a little."

In her own unique style, Pia was wearing a pastel green dress, the scarf she bought in China Town tied around her waist. The silky belt, painted with pink lotus blossoms, was her only adornment—no earrings or necklace, or hair clip. She made appearing beautiful seem easy.

"You look like spring," I told her.

"That's the idea. Ready?"

We walked along the same path we'd taken the night before. The reception drew friends and family of the artists, as well as Art Practice Department faculty. Department Head, Dr. James Ferguson, shook my hand and said, "Welcome to California." Matteo ignored Pia and me, offering only a slight nod as he mingled, ooh-ing and aah-ing loudly, as if he hadn't seen the show. I added fake enthusiasm to the case I was building against him. As more gallery goers trickled in, Pia migrated toward her work.

Despite Pia's pronouncement of the night before, Marilyn Wu, who painted songbirds, proved to be nice enough. She introduced me to her mother. Sensing someone else who didn't quite fit in, Mrs. Wu followed me around the gallery. We carried little cups of white wine, and stopped to examine each piece. Mrs. Wu definitely recognized my portrait. "The painter is your friend?" She looked back and forth from the wall to me.

"Yes." I nodded, wishing she wouldn't speak so loudly. Then I saw her identify the half-nude man on the wall as Matteo, who, in real life, was standing across the room and surrounded by students. She surprised me by walking in the opposite direction. Relieved she knew better than to create a scene, I followed. Alan, the painter of red flowers, stood alone under his amaryllis. "Very pretty," Mrs. Wu told him.

"Thank you." He held out his hand to her and they shook. He extended his hand to me. "Also very pretty." When he touched me, little warning bells went off. Instead of shaking, his hand caressed mine. "Hello, mysterious woman."

"Laura." I eased my hand away and waited for the flutters to stop. "I'm a friend of Pia's."

"Of course you are." He beamed, as if he said something brilliant. He leaned toward me, lifted my hair away from my ear, and whispered, "Come to dinner with me after the reception."

"Oh, I'd love to. Really. And, no."

"Okay. Are you busy for lunch tomorrow?"

"No."

"Meet me here around noon?"

"I can't go out with you."

"Laura, please, give me a chance." He flashed a beautiful smile.

"I-I'm, uh…" I searched for the right word to describe my relationship with Sam. "Involved."

"Oh, I see." He bowed at the waist, took my hand, and kissed it. "Lovely to meet you, my dear." Then he turned his attention to another couple who stood nearby, admiring his painting.

Rattled by sudden emotion, I said good bye to Mrs. Wu and sought Pia. She was standing with a small group of people directly under the portrait of me. When I walked over to them, they gave a soft little burst of applause, then wandered on. "Having fun?" Pia pulled me into a quiet alcove.

"Alan asked me out."

"I'll leave the key under the mat."

"What? You think I'm going?"

"Why not? He's a cool guy. Quite talented and smart."

"Sam."

"Excuse me?"

"That's why I'm not going."

"How would he find out? Certainly not from me."

I gave my head a toss of moderately righteous indignation. "That's not how I operate."

"You don't have enough experience to know how you operate."

"Oh, really?"

"Being loved and owned are different."

She was about to expound further when an art student, drawn by our voices, peeked into the alcove. "You might want to come out now. The sale stickers are going up."

Out in the gallery a mild storm was building. In a matter of seconds, I observed Mrs. Wu whisper into her daughter's ear. Looking toward Matteo's portrait, Marilyn whispered back. Mrs. Wu held Marilyn's arm and shook her head. Brushing off her mother's gentle restraint, Marilyn headed toward the back, where faculty members gathered. Desperate to avoid gale force winds, I intercepted her.

"Hello." Touching her shoulder, I introduced myself. "Your work is lovely. I'd like to buy your chickadees."

Forced to walk to the sale table to complete the transaction, she turned her attention away from Matteo to thank me. We followed a gallery assistant over to the painting and watched her apply a red dot on the placard. The reception closed at seven. Most folks with Saturday night dinner plans had already departed. Faculty went *en masse* down the hall to a banquet. All three of Pia's pieces bore little red stickers.

"Want to celebrate?" I took her arm. "My treat."

"Actually I'd just like to go home." Pia looked wilted.

Back at the apartment, I stuffed cheese and avocado into pitas. Shoes off, Pia curled into a ratty lawn chair on the tiny balcony and closed her eyes. I draped a shawl over her shoulders and handed her a plate of food. "Thanks." She took a bite. "For earlier, too."

"You would have done the same for me."

She nodded.

"My check will bounce," I told her.

"It's only fair for me to reimburse you. Happy early, early Birthday."

"I really like the painting."

"I know. Now you have a funny story to go with it."

"Funny?"

"Yeah. The one about your naïve friend."

"Glad to help out. What do you think would happen if Dr. Ferguson found out about you and Matteo?"

"Not much. Berkeley's gigantic. Fortunately, or unfortunately, student-teacher affairs are common." She stood up and stretched. "The wrong politics, on the other hand, might qualify for probationary measures." She pushed her plate away. "It doesn't matter, anyway. I'll end him soon."

"Good." I hoped I'd had something to do with her decision.

"I saw him ogling another student at the reception."

"Sounds like you're not into sharing."

"It's not that." She paused. "I wish I could have shared tonight's success with Charley. He would have stayed by my side, and still charmed everyone in the room. He had a way of being…" she looked up at the sky "…satisfied with life. And he made everyone else feel the same way. He would ask someone just the right question to get them comfortable, and, within five minutes, have a new friend."

"I wish I could have met him."

"Me, too." She started to clear the plates. "Matteo knows a lot about art, but he's shallow compared to my truck driver."

"By the way," she said once we were inside, "Professor Corselli bought himself."

I laughed. "Of course he did. I imagine he'll hang that portrait in his front hall, so all the women can see what they're in for when he takes his shirt off."

"No doubt." She paused. "Nick bought the picture of you."

"You're kidding."

"Nope. You're going to Hawaii. On paper, that is. He says you remind him how he was forced to give up his wayward youth."

"Cool. And the young Hawaiian girl?"

"She'll be on the cover of a book I'm writing with Tutu."

"That sounds totally fun."

"It was the only way I could get her to stop pestering me about everything. Sometimes I don't know whose life I'm living, hers, or mine."

I wanted to tell Pia I felt exactly the same way about my relationship with her. Instead I hugged her. "Thanks for bringing me to Berkeley."

When my return flight landed in Cincinnati, Sam kissed me on the lips and presented flowers. In the car, before he could ask about my trip, I lobbied for a visit to his folks, who lived nearby. "This wouldn't be good timing, Babe. Dad's in the middle of his campaign for municipal judge in Hamilton."

"We won't stay long. Seeing you would be a nice surprise."

"My dad isn't fond of surprises."

"Oh, come on." I play-punched his upper arm. "Let's be spontaneous."

Shaking his head, he started the car.

"You did tell them about us at Christmas, right?"

"Sure. They know I'm seeing someone."

"Seeing someone? That's what you're doing, Sam? Really?"

"Well, yeah." He turned the engine off.

"First." I really tried not to point, but my index finger scolded him. "We've been living together for the entire school year. Second, on Valentine's you said you loved me. We're a couple." I held up the bouquet, waving it in his face as proof. Sam stared out the car window and waited for the inevitable rest of the rant. "Hey. Guess what?" I taunted him to get his attention. "A guy in California asked me out. An artist."

Sam turned, and the hurt on his face made me regret using that ammunition.

"I didn't go, though." My hand found his shoulder. "I didn't go."

"Good."

"Sam, I need to meet your folks."

"Okay." He nodded and blew a little air out of his mouth. "We'll go for my birthday."

"All right." I scooted over next to him to give him a kiss on the cheek. "What about summer?"

"What about it?"

"Maybe I could stay with your family." I stroked his cheek. "We wouldn't have to separate." I'd hatched the plan on the plane ride home.

"Maybe." He didn't look at me.

"You can at least ask."

"I'll try." Sam started the car.

"Your best, right?"

"Let's play it by ear."

True to his word, Sam made the arrangement with his folks, which gave me six long weeks to dread something I asked for. "Should I tie my hair back when I meet your mom?"

"Whatever you want."

"Maxi skirt or bell bottoms?"

"Really, Laura, it doesn't matter." He sat on the bed.

"It matters to me." I stood in front of the mirror. "And, oh, what about a gift for the hostess? Should we take fresh tomatoes from farmer's market? Or chocolates? How about tea? Does your mother like tea?"

"Please stop, honey, you're getting all worked up over nothing." Placing two pillows behind his back, he leaned against the headboard.

"Nothing? Meeting your folks? You're way too relaxed, Sam."

"And you are much more pleasant when you are relaxed."

"I will be by the time we get there."

"So I've got six more weeks of you freaking out every day?"

"Freaking out? I'm asking your opinion, that's all."

"Here's my opinion. You're beautiful, polite, and have a great personality. Plus, you're smart."

"But am I good enough for their first-born?"

"Why would you even ask?"

"Pia's dead husband's family snubbed her. They made it clear from the start they did not approve."

Sam left the bed and crossed the room. "You always bring everything back to Pia."

"Not always, not everything."

"Well, that's the way it seems to me."

"She's my friend."

"And I'm not?" Sam pulled me close. "Trust me on this, okay?"

I nodded into his chest.

Sam's birthday fell on the first Saturday in May, Derby Day in Louisville. Mint juleps, made with fine Kentucky bourbon, spill into special silver cups. Horse racing fans and bettors wear hats and pay thousands for a box seat at Churchill Downs. Our friends would be in the infield sipping from miniature whiskey bottles. Those unable to attend would be hosting Derby parties, stopping to focus at the early evening post time on the two to three-minute Run for the Roses.

Sam and I were driving to Ohio in an oil-burning Studebaker. At the start of the trip I clenched my hands into fists, then released them, consciously and slowly, trying to relax. By the time we crossed into Ohio, my fingers sped up. The frantic flicks made a brushing sound. "Hey, Laura, please stop." Sam fooled with the car radio and got static.

"Sorry." I pressed the palms of my hands together.

"Let's play a game or something."

"No, thanks." I closed my eyes and wished for Pia in my pocket. She would help me make sense of my fears. "Of course, you're nervous," she had said, when we talked on the phone the week before. "It's stressful to meet your potential in-laws. Plus, you really have no idea what Sam has told them about your relationship."

"Well, he probably hasn't shared the fact that we're having sex, so undoubtedly we'll have separate rooms."

"They would do that anyway, Laura, even if they knew, or suspected. That's just parents. They don't want you mating under their roof."

"That makes us sound like animals."

"You are." She laughed. "Enjoy it while you can. The instinct doesn't last forever, you know."

"What's that supposed to mean?"

"Nothing. Just be horny and happy and don't get pregnant before you want to."

"The Pill adds a few pounds and some bloat," I said. "But worth it, though, for peace of mind."

"And piece of ass."

"You're funny today. Kind of giddy, actually. Are you stoned, like everyone else in Berkeley?"

"No, never touch the stuff." Pia paused. "Just happy."

"Have you replaced Matteo?"

"Uh-uh. Too busy."

"Not so lonely, then?" I wanted her to say how much she missed me, that she missed me at all.

"Nope. Teaching, drawing, trying to pass some core requirements like statistics. Nick and his family will land here for the summer, you and Sam in Ohio, and I'll come back to my house by the river and Kate Hall."

Remembering how her studio got its name, I smiled into the phone, as if she could see me. "That sounds great."

"And, by the way, Kevin's going to be around. Maybe you and Sam can drive down and spend a weekend or two."

"Sounds cool. All of us, mere pawns on the big chessboard of your life."

"What's that supposed to mean?"

"Nothing. Bad joke."

"The book I'm writing with Tutu takes a lot of my time. She dictates to Nick's wife, Nani, who types up these fantastic myths, then mails them to me illustrate."

"Please send me one. I'd love to see."

"Will do. Relax, enjoy your Sam, and tell him happy birthday from me. Big kiss." She hung up without waiting for my response.

Sam's mother, Sally Jennings, met us at the door with a big hug for her tall son and a warm greeting for me. "Hello, dear." She took both my hands in hers and made a warm little tent. Here was the person who had raised Sam, taught him to open doors, stand when a woman entered the room, and say please often. Like her son, she would be easy to love.

"Hello, Mrs. Jennings." Smiling, I relaxed my shoulders.

Two boys ran up behind her, and she released my hands to raise her palm, signaling them to stop.

"Sam-Sam-Sam." One child pushed forward and tried to climb Sam like a jungle gym.

"Hi there, Bill-Bill-Bill." Sam pushed his youngest brother down and patted the top of his head. The other boy, bigger, more polite, reached to shake his older brother's hand. In an instant, Sam put him in a gentle headlock. "Look sharp, Tom." Sam let him go and turned the boys to face me. "Guys, this is Laura."

"Hi," they said in unison.

Then a dog, a collie mix, bolted for the front door. She barked to greet Sam, who kneeled to pat her. "Sam," I said, "you didn't tell me your home life was just like 'Lassie.'" That sent the boys into giggles, and they ran circles around us.

"Boys, time to wash your hands for lunch. Bill, get your father from the garage. And Tom, find John. He's studying somewhere." Mrs. Jennings closed the front door. "Sam, show Laura to her room. We've put John in with you."

Sam picked up my little duffel bag and led me past the living room down a carpeted hall. He showed me to a clean, sparsely furnished room, quite obviously inhabited by a teenage boy. Farah Fawcett's dazzling smile shone down from a poster on a wood-paneled wall. A plaid bedspread, still warm from the dryer, covered military themed flannel sheets. Scouting and track trophies sat on pine bookshelves. A thinner, shorter Sam with glasses entered the room behind us.

"Hey, John." Sam and his brother punched arms. "This is Laura."

"Hi, Laura." John extended his hand for me to shake.

"Thanks for letting me use your room," I said.

"You're welcome. Mom says for you both to come to lunch."

Sam showed me the nearest bathroom. I washed my hands, finger-brushed my hair, and took a few deep breaths. *You're in, you're okay. It's going to be fine.*

By the time I joined the family at the table the atmosphere had changed. There was no pleasant chatter, just the clink of spoons against serving dishes as bowls were passed and plates served. All four Jennings boys and their father stood when I entered the room. Sam pulled out a chair for me.

"Dad, this is Laura."

"Hello." Judge Jennings made a slight nod in my direction before he sat again.

"Hello, Mr. Jennings."

"Would you like peas, dear?" Mrs. Jennings asked. Without waiting for an answer, she handed a bowl to John who passed it to Tom, who passed it to Sam.

"Mac and cheese," she said brightly, sending another dish on the same circuitous path. "Now that the boys are older, we eat our family meal at Saturday lunch. That way they're freed up in the evenings for their activities." She looked proudly around the table at her brood before picking up her fork. "Please eat, everyone. There's pie and ice cream for dessert."

Like the starting pistol at a track meet, her words brought instant motion.

"What kind of activities do you do?" I ventured to fill the silence, addressing the question to no one boy in particular.

"Scouts," the judge answered for them. "I expect all the boys to become Eagles."

Knowing absolutely nothing about scouting, with maybe the exception of a few of their laws to be trustworthy, loyal, and obedient, I didn't respond.

Sam picked up. "Dad leads the Ohio Camporee every year. Scouts from all counties meet up to learn survival skills."

I nodded. If we were having this conversation between just us, I would have engaged in a philosophical debate. Survival skills meant something different to me. A scout could tie all the knots in the world, but might never know how to put a drunken father to bed, or help a mother call a taxi. A scout might light a campfire, but not step away from the smoke. I knew how to get out of the woods before they burned. No one asked questions about my social activities. I wanted to tell them about their son and brother. That his poor grades didn't measure his intelligence. That he helped people. How we fit together.

The Jennings boys proceeded to tell me about their badges. Trying to read Judge Jennings' demeanor, I only half-listened. The man held his jaw tightly. He barely acknowledged his young sons' enthusiastic chatter. His eyes stayed on Sam, who waited for the boys to pause, then said, "Until Dad bought it ten years ago, the main house was part of a working farm."

"What crops grew here?" I asked, wanting to take part in the conversation.

"Oh some sorghum, a little corn," Sam answered. "We used to have a cool old barn, but it had to be scrapped." He finished his last bites. "Dry-rot."

"That old thing was an eyesore and fire hazard." Whenever Mr. Jennings spoke, silence followed.

I finished most of my meal and offered to help clear the table.

"That would be nice, dear," Mrs. Jennings murmured.

"May we please be excused?" John asked.

The patriarch nodded.

"What about pie?" Tom asked.

"We'll call you in a little while," his mother said. "Your father needs to speak with Sam."

My stomach lurched.

In the kitchen we made small talk while we loaded the dishwasher. My ears weren't keen enough to hear the conversation from the adjoining dining room. But when voices rose, I moved to the threshold and peeked in. "She'll get a job." Sam's impatience took the form of a loud exhale.

Judge Jennings shoved his chair back from the table to stand. "Out of the question," he barked.

"Summer's only three months. She can take my room. I'll share with John." Sam sounded like he was underwater. To show my support I stepped into the room and came up beside him, close, forcing him to slip his arm around me. *United front.*

"That makes me want to vomit." Judge Jennings hit his fist against the table. He looked at Sam. "There's no reason on God's green earth for your girlfriend to live here. What a bad example to set for your brothers. Think I want to have a harem by the time you're all teenagers?"

"No," Sam whispered. The fight had gone out of him.

"And, you...," Judge Jennings struggled for my name. "...Laura. What kind of parents would allow you to do such a thing?" Before I could muster an answer, he held up a hand. "Wait. Dumb question. They wouldn't know the truth of the matter, would they? In fact, I doubt they know you're visiting us this weekend. Why don't we call them?"

"Thanks," I managed. "I'll let them know right away."

"Phone's on the hall table." He pointed, waiting for me to move.

Sam took my hand and led me the opposite way, through the kitchen. We sat on the concrete steps outside the back door. By this time, I was crying, my cheeks prickling with humiliation. Judge Jennings was right. My plan sounded immature and self-centered. "Let's go home," I muffled into Sam's shirt.

"Baby, I can't." Sam's thumb stroked the tears away. "My birthday's tomorrow. They're my family."

"So?" I choked. More tears made talking impossible. "You should have warned me."

"Shh." He smoothed my hair. "Don't take Dad personally. In his house, you've got to follow his rules."

When we went back inside, the family was enjoying the promised dessert. The boys chattered. No one interrupted us as we entered John's room and closed the door. Sam lay down on the bottom bunk, motioning me to lie down on top of him. His gentle gesture quieted me. After my tears stopped, Sam said, "Be right back." Through the closed door I could hear the murmur of more discussion. Several minutes later he returned waving a key ring. "Dad loaned me his car." He seemed a little too happy and sort of proud. *Divide and conquer.*

On the road home, Sam turned on the radio. "I'll be back early. Promise. Mom's made a special cake, and Tom and Bill get all excited about the candles. The main meal's lunch, as usual." He patted my thigh.

Up until now, marrying Sam had meant the chance for another set of parents, a competent mom, a loving father. Granted, in Sam's mind we weren't close to the altar, but summer under his roof would make our next step obvious. I saw myself as a help to his mother, especially with chores and watching the younger boys. I imagined discussing politics with his dad, maybe even going on a hike with the Scouts. As my fantasies vanished, new ones arose. Now Sam and I would be star-crossed lovers. We'd graduate, get jobs, marry, move out on our own. In real life, Sam deposited me at Pia's and headed back to his family.

Exhausted by disappointment, I went to bed early and slept until dawn. The chirping of spring birds woke me, and I couldn't help but feel cheerful. It had been a long time since I'd been alone. I slipped a sweatshirt over my pajamas and made coffee. Outside, the steam from my mug made a private little cloud for me to follow. Walking, I searched for the stones Pia placed Thanksgiving before last. Most of the round river rocks had tumbled downhill, straying from any kind of order. Eventually, I came to the small clearing where Pia had chanted to the strange bundle.

Imitating her motions, I lifted my arms and turned my face to the sky. In the branches of a nearby tree, the royal blue bundle rested, alongside a purple one. Nestled beside it was another object. Squinting up into the half-light, I used a branch to prod the strange bag from its nest, and it landed near my feet. Curious, and a little scared, I bent to touch the cylindrical shape. Whatever was inside felt soft and pliable. I recognized the outer cloth, printed with flowers, as Pia's blouse I had worn the night of my makeover, the night we waited for Kevin to bring a friend. The sleeves of the shirt, knotted together loosely, would open with a gentle tug. I could peek inside without her knowing. But I didn't. Instead, I climbed up on the highest boulder and replaced the bundle between the V of the branches. My spirit could stay put for a while longer.

In the house, I puttered, picking up and folding clothes, preparing a birthday dinner for Sam. Around noon, Pia called. "How'd the big meet up go?"

"Okay."

"Really, Laura, you must have more to say."

"His brothers are really cute. They have a great collie."

"What about Mom and Dad?"

"Warm and intimidating, in that order. Listen, I can't talk right now. Jan's coming over for a study session." My lie reminded me of the times I covered for her when Nick called.

Later that night, when Sam returned, a new Laura greeted him. The bundle in the tree made me think about keeping certain things inside. By unspoken agreement, we didn't talk about his family. I gave him his birthday gift, a keychain engraved with his initials, the ones I wrote over and over in the margins of my notebooks. During the next month we fell into a sweet routine of daily life, without my usual insistence on discussing every detail. My confidence in us grew. We might sail over this wave after all. In my mind I defended myself to Judge Jennings again and again.

"Sam loves me," I would say. "We want to be together." But the facts didn't change. The approaching summer would mean Sam in Ohio without me. His parents would encourage him to date other girls. Worse, he might want to.

Pia planned to return by mid-June, and she would turn Kate Hall into a classroom. Her new brochure detailed the classes she would teach. Even though I knew I'd be welcome, the house would be full of children eating sandwiches at lunchtime and adults munching hors d'oeuvres in the evenings. Pia believed in feeding her students, literally. "We'll have all that fruit from still-life week."

I ignored her little joke.

"You can be my art assistant." Pia paused. "In trade for room and board."

"Thanks, that's generous. But I need to work this summer." My financial situation bordered on desperate. I wished to stay there, where I'd made my home for nearly two years, but knew I had to push myself to try something new.

My opportunity came, unexpectedly, one day during Advanced Brit Lit class. Dr. Dorothy Bucks, secretly called Dottie by her students, held a special fondness for me. We shared a passion for Shakespeare. "You have a gift for understanding the Bard's symbol and nuance, Laura," Dr. Bucks told me. "Please consider staying on campus this summer to assist with my manuscript." My outer, growing-up Laura smiled and said yes, my inner child nearly jumped herself into a fainting fit.

Sam and I kissed good-bye with vows to write and visit, reminding each other it wasn't all that far. I knew the distance would be emotional. With the help of a fellow English major, I cleaned Pia's house and packed up my things. I moved into one of the dorms, near the room I'd lived in as a freshman and pined for Patrick. In many ways, I was starting over.

Dr. Bucks, an elegant woman nearing sixty, wore her grey hair pulled into a neat bun. Most summer days, she wore a tailored linen jacket over a sleeveless blouse, and a straight skirt that emphasized her trim figure. Her perfect speech, always grammatically correct, sometimes made me feel awkward. Striving to impress her, I wore conservative clothes and no eyeliner, my long hair pulled back in a low pony tail, tied with plain grosgrain ribbon. My flowered scarves wilted in a suitcase.

She needed to publish by the end of the year. "November, if possible," she said. "Remember, Laura, 'Strong reasons make strong actions.'"

"*King John*," I said.

"Yes." She smiled "Precisely why I chose you for the job."

Our work schedule meant early mornings, meals next to the typewriter, and long hours in several university libraries. While I drove, she would read parts of her thesis aloud. Working for Dr. Bucks also meant that I ordered and picked up research materials at the small bookstore in town. Deliveries came at least three times a week, and one afternoon the owner greeted me. "Hello, Shakespeare Girl." His British accent made him seem worldly. "A Stratfordian, judging by the books you order."

Tongue-tied in his presence, I didn't know enough to get involved in a discussion. "Not me, my prof."

He came out from behind the counter and extended his hand, "Ian Harrington."

"Laura McKenna."

"Oh, you're Irish, then?"

I laughed at his earnestness. "Way, way, way back, yes, but nobody I know got off a boat."

"Good. Who's your prof?"

"Dr. Dorothy Bucks."

"Ah, yes, of course, Dottie's at it once more. Every few years or so the academics must publish. And it gets harder for them because...," he leaned toward me to whisper, "...there's nothing new under the sun." He stepped back behind the counter, chuckling, pleased with his witticism, which I didn't really get, but wasn't about to say so. Late twenties, I guessed. Beatles' hair, a light sandy color, flopped into his face. His glasses didn't quite fit, and he kept pushing them back up when they scooted down his nose. Ian wasn't really good-looking, but his features were pleasant.

Flattered by his attention, I leaned forward. "Are her books ready?"

"Indeed they are." He wrapped three slim volumes in brown paper, taking great care to fold each corner precisely, studying me while doing so. His fingers were long and quick. When he finished, he came around the counter and bowed his head, presenting the packet to me as if it were precious jewelry. "Anything else?" He pursed his lips.

Maybe it was my imagination, but I heard a come-on. For the slightest fraction of a moment I considered flirting, but convinced myself that Sam and I were in a sweet spot.

Ian might be worth the risk. "No, thanks, not today."

He walked me out to Dr. Bucks' car and, borrowing the keys, opened the door for me. "Be good now, pet." He gently closed the door. I drove around the corner, parked the car, and swooned.

On Sunday I helped Pia. The studio, overflowing with partially finished canvasses, smelled oily. We cleaned brushes, dusted easels, tossed half-used charcoal pencils in the trash. Our brief chats didn't touch into deeper subjects. My conversations with Sam also suffered. He didn't want to hear about Shakespeare, I didn't ask about his family, job, or what else he might be doing. We weren't off, but less than on.

The next time errands took me to Madison, I wore a summer dress, soft cotton, no bra. The outfit had the desired effect on Ian Harrington. He beamed at me through the glass window of the bookstore. Before I got to the door, he swooped around the corner to greet me. "Hello again, Miss McKenna." Instead of shaking my hand, he walked straight toward me, stopped less than a foot away and gazed at my bare shoulders. "Hot, is it?"

Again I heard the innuendo, and responded in kind. "Getting hotter by the minute." As soon as I spoke, I felt foolish.

He took a tiny step closer. "Dottie's books aren't in yet."

I took several steps back. "My mistake."

"Right." He went back behind the counter.

On the way out, I wondered what Ian thought of me, but what I thought of myself mattered more. Sam's flirtations wounded me. Why should mine be acceptable? The first hand lesson in double standard made me anxious for summer to end, for Sam and me to get back to our routine. Routines were, by definition, predictable. And predictable meant safe. For the next month, I called ahead to make sure the books had come in. I'd wait until Ian went to lunch and deal with his assistant. Mistress of avoidance, I tucked away my summer dresses until Sam returned to school.

At the end of August Sam moved back to his fraternity house, and I moved to the dorm next to faculty housing. Dr. Bucks continued to need my assistance in the evenings, and it was easier if I lived nearby. Suddenly we were seniors, the reality nothing like my previous fantasy. Sam and I, married, living off campus in a darling little house on the edge of town; Pia, helping us decorate, would choose wonderful paint colors, the perfect furniture. I'd have gardens for both flowers and food. A few select couples would visit us for dinner parties. "You grew the roses yourself? The spinach is from your garden? Incredible." I could hear them in my mind. Deep conversation would follow. Politics, Literature, Human Rights.

Instead, Sam and Pia were increasingly distant satellites to Planet Laura. Between senior classes, writing an undergrad thesis, and working for Dottie Bucks, I barely slowed. When I did, I briefly pondered how I could be living so separately from the two people I loved most in the entire world.

One Saturday evening in the fall Sam asked me to a dance at his frat house. Normally I avoided these events because I didn't find the atmosphere appealing. Loud music, booze, guys and girls in various stages of undress, publicly groping. But this was Hippie Dance, first dance of our senior year, and he seemed sentimental about it, so I said yes.

We dressed in matching tie-dyed shirts and bright pink bell bottoms. In spite of the Midwestern chill, we went barefoot. Sam walked me up to the second floor. Decorations included peace signs and rainbows made with paper plates and glitter. *In-A-Gadda-Da-Vida* blasted from huge speakers. Strobe lights flashed across the revelers, most heading toward drunkenness. Everything smelled like beer. "Cool, huh?" Sam kept my hand as we went to the dance floor.

I squinted and blinked, attempting to match my eyes to the rhythm of the bursts of color. A girl dressed in a leather mini skirt made swimming movements toward us and dropped a strand of love beads over Sam's head. She gave him a deep French kiss, moving her pelvis into his. His hands cupped her butt and pulled her closer. I turned and left the party. Sam followed, took my hand, and led me up the stairs. Girls weren't allowed on the third floor, but the housemother and other chaperones were at the dance. Guiding me into his bedroom, he shut the door. When he tried to hug me, I pulled away, crossing my arms over my chest. My emotions see-sawed between anger and hurt. Not trusting myself to speak, I took a deep breath or two, waiting to hear him out.

"Not my fault Denise likes me." Sam shrugged.

"You know her?"

"Well, yeah. She hangs around the House a lot." He paused. "After school, before dinner. Helps out with duties."

I heard about local high school girls who idolized frat boys. "You mean she gets passed around the House a lot."

Without protest or defense, Sam nodded.

"You've made out with her before."

He nodded again. "Everybody has. Does."

"Who invited her tonight?"

"I thought she'd have fun."

"How considerate. Scout Law, right?" I opened the door. "Time to go."

"I'll drive you." Sam put on his slippers and picked up his keys.

Because I was barefoot, I didn't argue. "Wait here a second," I said, when he pulled up in front of the dorm. Two minutes later I climbed into the front seat and gave him back his pin.

"Laura, I'm sorry." He turned the pin over in his hand. "Are you sure this is what you want?"

I paused. "What do you want?" Afraid to hear his answer, I looked out the car window.

"I don't know."

Not as bad as I thought. I turned toward him. "Well, at least you're being honest." The tears I had been holding back began. "Another Scout Law." I sniffed, offering a weak smile.

"You have all these plans." He moved his hands in the air, as if clearing cobwebs. "I'm not ready to get married and have no idea what to do after graduation." He slipped an arm around me, and I let him. Explaining that he was "still a kid at heart," and "wasn't ready for real life," Sam ended us with one last hand-squeeze.

In my dorm room, I pulled back the curtain to see if he waited or changed his mind, but the Studebaker was gone. Soon my first lover would be making out with one of the extra girls at the dance. Minus the eyeliner and hippie costume, wearing a pair of flannel pajamas, I sat in bed and hugged my knees. Sam's spiel made the good-bye easier. His qualities, the ones that initially attracted me, proved to be the same ones that drove me away. Friendliness, not to me in particular, to everyone. His devotion transformed into obligation, and spontaneity became an excuse to keep the party going. The few times he expressed curiosity were without passion. *Plain vanilla.* My thoughts helped me fend off heartbreak for about an hour, before I cried myself to sleep.

News travelled fast on our small campus. Within a few days everyone knew we were no longer a couple. In the back of the library, seeking no comfort, sympathy, or strength from others, I buried myself in work. Defeat was mine alone. When Patrick proposed, I withdrew to my private island, until Pia invited me onto hers. If I went to her now, she would offer perceptive insight and explain the ways of men. But I preferred to remain in retreat. No explanation could soothe me. Nothing would ever be all right again.

Over the next two weeks, emotional blinders in place, I devoted my time to Dr. Bucks, or my own studies. Applying for student teaching placement, I chose distant towns, far enough away to escape campus living, and reminders of Sam. Jeffersonville, Indiana, directly across the river from Louisville, fit the bill, even though it meant moving home with my parents. *Could my life get any worse?*

The daily drive across the bridge frightened me, and I would arrive at school, stomach churning, as I had in first grade. The drab, reddish-gray building, built at the turn of the century, stood in the center of town. Large windows, tops arched, were intended to be graceful. Now, cloudy grime made them unattractive and non-functional. Heavy doors completed City School's uninviting features. Inside, traditional classrooms, large blackboards in front and hefty podiums for teachers to hide behind, separated from students, held about forty desks. Over the years, penciled initials and notes wore grooves on their tops. None of them looked clean, despite obvious efforts to bleach and scrub the markings away. The halls smelled of ammonia-over-sweat, the bathrooms of air freshener, and the Teacher's Lounge of coffee and cigarettes.

My supervising teacher, Mrs. Martin, a frumpy woman, fiftyish, wore bright red lipstick and thick glasses. She'd chosen me from a list of seven applicants, based on my experience with Shakespeare. "Mind you, Miss McKenna," she said during my interview, "reading the Bard isn't teaching him, especially to teenagers." Emotions out of balance, I forced myself to pause. Quite possibly I knew more than she did, and would make a better teacher, but this was the time to play humble. "Yes, ma'am."

My ninth-grade students, whip-smart in ways beyond book learning, knew all about inner turbulence. The two morning classes, English I R were Remedial; afternoon classes, English I A, Advanced. Tracking students into intellectually homogenous groups made teaching easier for the teacher, less challenging for the student. The syllabus for each class was identical, including writing skills, oral expression, and reading *Romeo and Juliet*. I had eight weeks to get a hundred and twenty fourteen-year-olds to understand five acts of unrhymed iambic pentameter.

As far as I could tell, Mrs. Martin owned two suits, one navy blue, the other gray, which she alternated. The buttoned jackets covered her thick waist, and I suspected the mid-calf skirts hid plump thighs and knees. The first week she sat in the back of the classroom while I taught. After that, she'd greet me in the morning, and say goodbye in the afternoon. Occasionally, she'd open the classroom door and peek in, rotating her head to scan for trouble, and say: "If you need me, I'll be in the Lounge." I would nod, careful not to interrupt the lesson, and briefly wonder what kind of situation would require her intervention.

Challenged to learn names, I memorized the roll-call lists at home. Certain kids would do better up front, but Mrs. Martin forbade any change to the seating charts. My idea to rearrange the desks in a circle when we read aloud didn't fly either. I settled for readers standing in the front of the room, eyes glued to the text, struggling with Elizabethan English and poor lighting.

My work satchel rode along on the front seat. Home by four in the afternoon, I'd make a sandwich and retreat to my room before my parents began drinking. I'd spread papers out over my sister's twin bed, and, red pen in hand, sit on the floor. Plusses, checks, or zeroes trailed beside each name in the grade book. Most of the kids were pretty good about turning in simple homework assignments. All but one, whose name was the first I'd learned.

Mrs. Martin advised me to ignore him. "Curtis isn't much trouble. He'll sleep through class, and you best let him." She shivered in mock terror. "Don't pick a fight with a kid his size." She shook her head. "He's close to sixteen. Failed my class two years in a row. Never picked up a pencil."

First period started at 7:30 am, and most students dozed through roll call. What I didn't know, and had to figure out all by myself, was that several students in Remedial were not there for lack of intelligence, but for lack of food and shelter. Foster

Children, Juvenile Delinquents, Under-Achievers, the labels rotated through a variety of words that meant Loser. Faculty Lounge gossip often included tales of their exploits. "Hear about Griffin? In juvie again over the weekend. Stole doughnuts. Caught with his fat hand on the chocolate-covered."

"Growing boy." A male teacher, helping himself to his own doughnut, laughed. "Fosters can't afford to feed him."

Defying Mrs. Martin, I moved Curtis to a chair right in front of my desk. A black kid, with large eyes and a full mouth, he had such trouble folding himself into a student desk, pencil and paper would have made him flip over. I saw no reason to fear him. Instead, I made space for him to write. Although his long arms easily reached the bigger surface, Curtis still would not participate. The minute an assignment was given, he would slump over into an immediate nap.

The day I handed him an apple, Curtis said, "Hey, Miss Mack, you got this all wrong." He handed the fruit back to me. "You're the teacher."

I shook my head. "For you. Have some raisins, too." I handed him a box with a picture of a smiling woman, the Sun Maid.

Curtis stared at the red box in his brown hand. "Do you think she's pretty?"

"Do you?"

"Sort of."

"Tell you what." I offered him a pencil. "Sit down and write your thoughts about her."

A half hour later he handed in a paper written in legibly printed uppercase letters.

HER SKIN AND SMILE ARE WHITE. HER HAIR IS DARK AND CURLY. THE SUN SHINES BEHIND HER DAY OR NIGHT. SHE'S GIVING GRAPES FROM HER BASKET TO ALL THE CHILDREN FOR FREE.

"Curtis, from now on I'll give you pictures to write about."

From then on, he kept writing, surprising everyone, including Mrs. Martin. It seemed like such a small gesture, handing a boy a box of raisins.

Two years earlier, Franco Zeffirelli had released a film that made Romeo and Juliet seem real, and the star-crossed lovers gazed from a poster in my classroom. Young, raven-haired Juliet wore red velvet and gold brocade. Romeo glowed with teenage lust. Soon all the kids were into writing about those classic faces. Some days I would check a record player out of the school library and play excerpts from the soundtrack. The kids' perfect imitations included British accents.

"Do you bite your thumb at us," instead of "up yours" echoed in the hallway outside my classroom. I invented games with Shakespeare's words. They giggled over "naked weapons," "kitchen wench," and "bosom." Mercutio won their hearts. They cried more over his death than Romeo's. Was Juliet's duty to her father, or to her new-found love? Had Sam asked himself the same question?

Marriage now struck me as the crux of most of the world's problems, especially mine. The see-saw of desire, possessiveness, and potential for betrayal would be non-existent without matrimony. My mother wouldn't have lived with an addict or suffered through shock treatments. Pia's whole life would have unfolded so differently had she not married a man ten years her senior who became an invalid and drug user. I wouldn't have wasted time wondering what was wrong with me when Pat wouldn't touch me. Sam couldn't have hurt me so. Juliet and Romeo could have carried on a discreet affair and run off to Naples.

The real test for a student teacher involves a classroom visit from one of the education department heads. My prof warned us that he would appear one day, unannounced. "Always make sure you are prepared and your students are prepared." Fairly late in the play, Act V, Scene I, Dr. Maricle showed up at the end of the school day, sixth period, to evaluate my teaching of English I A, Advanced. The students in this class were often rowdy, an indication of their intelligence more than rudeness. Somehow they were able to read and interpret text quickly, giving them time to act up.

My classrooms tended to be busy with noise and activity, some academic, some social. The kids in this group bounced back and forth without missing a beat.

"They're teenagers, and married!"

"My cousin Amanda just got married. She's only sixteen."

"*Had* to get married you mean."

"Juliet wasn't pregnant, was she?"

My back was to the class when Dr. Maricle walked in, but, in an instant, I knew something was up, because the room suddenly grew quiet. I turned around to find students sitting up straight, a few hands in the air. "Yes, Tracy." I called on one of the brightest girls.

"Now that we've past the climax in Act Three, is the remainder of the play considered anti-climax?"

"Good question." I watched Dr. Maricle make a note. "In a way. Sometimes everything that happens after the climax is called anti-climax. Even though there's more action to come, it's downhill from there. Some people say the anti-climax in this play comes in Act Five, so hold your thoughts until we finish the play."

Stevie raised his hand. I wanted to ignore him, but couldn't. Throughout the weeks he'd been a handful, speaking out of turn, getting perfect test scores, rarely doing homework. Our relationship wasn't combative, but we certainly weren't friendly. "Yes, Stevie?"

"Is the third word on the vocab list 'apothecary'?"

He has the vocabulary list? "Yes."

"Did you want us to use it in an original sentence?"

He's asking about an assignment? "Yes. Choose any five words. Remember, everyone, definitions due tomorrow."

The class period continued in the same vein. The kids made me look good.

On the last day of my student teaching, the first period class surprised me with a dozen red roses. When the bell rang, they waved good-bye and said thank you, except for Curtis. He sat, a solid mountain, in his chair as the next class came and filled the desks around him. "Curtis." I tapped a pencil on his arm. "Party's over. You have to go now."

"No ma'm." He shook his head.

"Second period's here."

"I know." He kept staring at me.

"What's the matter, Curtis?"

"Miss Mack?"

"Yes?" I leaned toward him.

"Miss Mack?"

I leaned closer. The kids, taking advantage of my inattention, were chatting, and I could barely hear Curtis over the hubbub.

"I paid good money for those roses."

"Thank you, Curtis." Feeling guilty for accepting any contribution from him, I reached under my desk for my purse.

"And I'd like to see a tear in your eye." He searched my face for evidence of emotion. "Also, I have a present for you." He handed me an envelope.

"This isn't really necessary."

"Oh, yes it is, Miss Mack." He stood and watched me remove tissue paper.

Inside was a Polaroid. Curtis, in the front room of his foster home, making a peace sign, looking like he owned the world.

"Remember me." Noticing the tears in my eyes, he nodded once, and shuffled out the door.

Right before Christmas, I turned twenty-one. In the past, I had fantasies about this special birthday. My parents would offer an extraordinary present. "Laura, we're so proud of you." Imaginary Father would put his arm around me. "And we love Sam." Make-Believe Mom would wave an envelope. "Two tickets. Anywhere." Of course we'd fly to Hawaii.

Another birthday dream starts with cocktails at the bar in the historic downtown Brown Hotel. The sound of cool jazz filters through gentle low hums of intimate conversation, and Sam lifts his glass. "To my darling." The lights of Louisville, not strobes, gently twinkle, catching a thin sheen of frost on the leafless trees in an innocent glisten. Candles on the table cast a soft glow, flattering my face, and highlighting the bodice of my low-cut, sequined evening dress. Our waiter presents a Private Menu. Sam, with the help of Chef, has selected exotic, sensual food for the Perfect Dinner. We taste, lingering over dessert and Irish coffee, until Sam pulls out a room key. "Let's go upstairs, sweetheart."

Instead, my parents took me to their country club, where Dad was well known, especially at the bar. The black wait staff fawned over him. With each drink, he became more patronizing. "Hon" for the women, "Bud" for the men. Embarrassment ate at my gut. The thick, quilted skirt of my dress, a relic from high school days, made me look like a displaced flower child. In a hurry to celebrate legal drinking age, I downed a sticky, sweet White Russian before dinner.

Excusing myself after a few bites into an appetizer, I fled to the ladies' room. The girl who stared back at me from the large, ornate mirror looked pale, almost haggard, and thin, not the picture of a healthy, college co-ed in her prime. I blamed Sam. After he left, I stopped taking the pill, and my puffy places melted away.

Eventually, I would make love to someone else, and have to teach my no-longer-soft body to respond, train my hands to trace another boy's jaw line, invent new pillow talk. I wondered if Sam compared me to Caftan Girl when they had sex. I wondered if he remembered how good we were, how right.

Soon I would need to face Pia. Over the last few months, she'd been sending letters, first from Berkeley, then from home, enclosing lovely drawings of new snow, a winter bird outside her window, an indoor herb garden we'd planted. And her usual elegant script: *Miss you, See you when you're ready. Me ke aloha pumehana, with the warmth of my love.*

The ladies room door opened, and Mom came in. She put her purse down on the counter and stood beside me in the mirror. "Honey, are you okay?" She started to apply fresh, red lipstick.

Unable to share my thoughts with her, I nodded.

"I can't believe my little girl is an adult, about to graduate from college, already teaching."

"Thanks, Mom." Accepting her praise, I took a breath, then put my hand on her arm. "We should get back to the table." We exchanged a look that said Dad shouldn't be left to order any more booze. During dessert, when other patrons and the waiters joined in singing Happy Birthday, I made three wishes: Sam back, a teaching job, reunion with Pia.

Before returning to campus, I walked from the main road down Pia's drive. The snowplow had been there. I was wearing new birthday boots, more for fashion than snow, but they kept my feet warm and had enough tread to prevent slipping. Smoke snaked from the chimney. As I lifted my hand to knock, Pia pulled me inside. "Come on." She closed the door fast and swept me into a hug. "Happy Late Birthday. You don't look a day over twenty." She smiled at her own joke.

"How did you know it was me?" I removed my gloves, but kept my coat on.

"Seriously?"

"Oh, that's right, I forget you have *juju* from your grandmother."

"God, it's so good to see you."

Slipping off my boots, I curled up in my favorite chair.

"Wait a sec and I'll make us hot toddies, now that you're legal and all."

She bustled in the kitchen and returned with two steaming mugs. "Whiskey, honey, and lemon juice." She handed me a mug. "Oh, and a little hot water. Just a little."

I took a sip. "We should have kept a list of all the special drinks we've had."

"Take your coat off." She hovered over me while I undid the buttons, then scooped the jacket out of my lap and trotted off to the bedroom. She returned with fuzzy slippers. "Put these on." Sure that I was comfortable, she moved to the couch across from me. "Tell me everything."

Starting with what had happened with Sam's dad, I continued on to the story of Caftan Girl, and paused only to sip the powerful, hot drink. My tale ended with student teaching Shakespeare. Pia listened, remaining still throughout most of an hour. Finishing, I took another swallow of the toddy, and set my cup down. "That's my sob story."

"Look at you." Her shoulders rose slightly, she turned her palms up. "All grown up, inside and out." Pia sounded as if she was bragging about her own child.

"Why do people keep saying that? Grown-up is the last thing I feel."

"Well, for one, you aren't actually sobbing. Also, the way you talk about those kids. You get what it means to want something for somebody else more than yourself."

Responding to her praise, I sat up a little straighter. "What about you? You must be heading back to California soon."

"To Kauai, actually." She wrapped both hands around her mug and drank. "For a while. Tutu's ailing. In fact..." she took another sip, "I may be gone for a few months."

"I'm so sorry, I didn't know."

"In the fall, she caught a cold that turned into bronchitis. A cousin from Honolulu is there now, but has to return to her own family soon. So I said I'd help out."

"What about Berkeley?"

"It will be there for a long time, she won't."

I nodded.

"Good timing is essential."

"Yes. I mean, I'm learning."

"You've stayed away from me for months."

A list of defenses rose to my lips, but Pia went on. "Avoiding my fatal flaws."

I couldn't tell if she was serious. "Like what?"

"Telling you how things are, instead of letting you live them yourself. Holding up my experience as expertise. Pushing you when you're uncomfortable."

"You would have encouraged me to confront Sam."

"Probably. I tend to shove you, rather than set you in motion. I've had to be such a fighter. First at home, then in my marriage, especially with Charley's family." She kept busy as she spoke, clearing our cups and straightening a pile of sketchbooks. "It sounds like rationalizing when I hear myself talk."

"Well, even if we don't see each other, you live in my head." I hesitated. "And I guess you keep me in that flowered blouse out in the trees."

"Ah." She sat. "You found your bundle." She turned her head to the side, as a bird might listen. "When?"

"A while ago."

"You've managed to keep a secret from me." She leaned back and laced her fingers together. "More than one."

"Well, not really. I'm telling you now, so they're not secrets anymore." I leaned back and crossed my legs. "Technically."

"You're right. I get it. And I'm glad you're thinking for yourself."

"Like I didn't before?"

"What do you think's in there?" She answered my question with one of her own.

"Tell me."

"The bundles are only for good, you know."

"I sensed that." I recalled my reverence in the clearing. "Although it surprised me to find more than one."

"A little history lesson. In old Hawaii ancestor worship could be dangerous." She drew little pictures with her hands in the air, as if playing charades. "Only a designated caretaker," she pointed to herself, "could communicate with the spirits who lived inside sacred bundles." She mimed speaking to an invisible bundle. Then she placed her ear to it and shook her head.

I thought of the stories my mother told me, about my dead grandmother in a casket in the front of the church. About ancestors who haunt you, bundles or not.

"Christianity forced them into hiding, tending in secret, sometimes letting the spirits loose to do harm, like bats from a cave, at dusk."

I thought of my mother's religion, unable to protect her from her fears.

"When I was a little girl, maybe five, Tutu warned me about the night-marchers, who still dress in ceremonial costumes and carry bundles along the ancient trails near her home in Kauai." Pia stood up and paced. "If you catch sight of them, they can take your soul." Swooping toward me she reached out with both hands.

"Like possess you?" Startled, I shrank back in the chair.

"Yes." She went back to the couch. "The only way to escape is to take off your clothes, lie down, and pretend to sleep."

My mother's shock treatments.

"Did you ever see any?"

"I heard them. Thunder came from their old drums, lightning from their torches."

"You must have been terrified."

"Tutu found me outside in the pouring rain. I hadn't been able to get my nightgown off over my head by myself, and it twisted around my neck. When she touched my shoulder to wake me, I screamed hysterically."

I saw myself, a young child, watching my mother attempting to wake my father, passed out on the family room couch.

Pia continued. "She scooped me up and put me in a warm bath. Then she sang me to sleep, rocking me in her arms and singing the old, sacred chants. By the next morning Tutu had created spirit children and showed me my bundle."

"By the time my mother was five," I said, "my grandmother was already a spirit. All my dreams about her were nightmares. I've always blamed her for my mother's depresssion, but lately I've been wondering if that's fair, if there's any difference between family history and ancestor worship."

"Not much. Both are full of myth, legends used to control our behavior and shape our morality. Tutu's bundles came into being for protection, to ward off possession."

"And to make you feel safe," I added. "All through childhood I wished for that."

"Oh, Laura." Pia's voice softened. "I've never felt safe. Right after Charley's accident, I made my first bundle. I'd stand in the clearing for hours and sing myself hoarse, hoping to lessen his pain." She shook her head. "Sound crazy?"

"Not really." I thought for a moment. "More like part superstition, part prayer. Catholics diminish sin through Indulgences, Hindus burn off karma to be reborn as a more conscious being. Are they any crazier?"

Pleased with my answer, Pia smiled. "Each spirit child can be unfastened using a pattern of knots Tutu showed me. I stuffed pills into Charley's bundle, along with my breath, hoping he could draw from my life force."

"The purple one must be his."

Wiping tears from her eyes with her sleeve, Pia nodded. "I still add drawings and written prayers. I open his bundle to the sun, so he doesn't have to stay in the dark all the time. I whisper my love for him, tell him all about you."

The hurt of breaking up with Sam could never compare with Pia's loss. I searched for words.

"Sometimes," Pia whispered, "I still get scared of night marchers."

The energy in the room, charged with our nostalgia, shifted as soon as the phone rang. At first, Pia didn't move. On the fifth or sixth ring she ran to answer. Pulling an afghan onto my lap, I nestled back into the chair, listening as Pia's half of the conversation drifted from the kitchen. "You're where? Wonderful. Can't wait to see you."

Pia rushed into the living room. "Nick and his family have been in the Bay Area, and are on their way here." She began to tidy up.

"That's great." I got up and folded the blanket over the back of the couch. Gathering my jacket and scarf, I reached for my boots.

"They won't get in until the wee hours. Why not spend the night? He'd love to see you."

"Really?" I fussed with the zipper on my boots. "I haven't seen Nick since his drug days, when we dumped his stash up at IU."

She smiled. "I remember."

"So will he."

"He does, asks about you all the time, bears no ill will."

"Ha." I didn't believe her.

"Once Tutu got a hold of him, our escapade seemed trivial. He's had many reparations to make. Now he wants to set things right with you."

"And how will he go about that?"

"Stick around and see for yourself."

Curiosity, and the fact that I felt more at home than I had in months, made me stay.

Pia's singing woke me. In the living room, I found Nick, loading the wood stove. "Laura." He stood and kissed my cheek. "Nani's making pancakes. Pia's entertaining the baby." We heard her laugh. "Or maybe it's the other way around."

"Good morning." Pia bounced into the room. "We're playing horsey." She brought the baby over to me. When I reached for his chubby hand, he reached back. His skin was a soft brown, his hair deep black. Dark eyes peeked out from under long velvety eyelashes. "He's gorgeous. What's your name, little one?"

"*Haloa* means long life. We call him Baby Hal." Nick beamed. At the sound of his father's voice, the boy turned toward Nick, who gently took Hal in his arms. Pia headed back to the kitchen. "He looks a lot like Nani, really. You'll see in a minute."

"There's a strong dose of you in there, though."

"I hear you're no longer a minor."

"True."

"So many changes in the last two years." Nick looked at the baby, then toward me. "For all of us." His wide grin told me all was forgiven. "First birthday next week, and we'll be at Tutu's, with Pia, to celebrate."

I felt a twinge of jealousy.

Nick opened the door and grabbed his jacket. "Tell them the guys will be outside." He bundled the baby into a fuzzy blanket. "Save us some breakfast."

The two women, laughing when I came in, didn't immediately hear me. From behind, Nani looked like Pia, only curvier. Her glossy black hair ran down her back in a long braid. They both turned. "Laura, *makamaka.*" Pia took both my hands in hers and guided me to the counter. "Meet Nani, wife of Nick, and mother of the world's most beautiful boy."

Nick was right. Hal had his mother's eyes. "Aloha, Laura," she said, wiping her hands on a dish towel before extending hers to me. A true Islander, she moved like wind through the palms. She spoke softly, punctuating English with Hawaiian, her movements making the words easy to understand.

"They decided to come for me, so we all could travel together." Pia, her love apparent, glowed. Shoulders relaxed, stance open, she had an ease I'd rarely seen. She belonged.

Throughout the day, we ate and visited. Pia spent time entertaining Baby Hal in the studio by painting faces on her fingers and his. Late afternoon, as I was leaving, Nani showed me a photograph of Tutu, a small cocoa colored woman with lovely, smooth skin, in a wicker chair on the front porch of a house surrounded by plumeria bushes. A long, white braid trailed over her shoulder. I studied her eyes, hoping to catch a hint of wisdom, but the photograph didn't convey the insights her grandchildren shared with me.

"Tutu wants to meet you in person." Nani tapped the picture. "Says she has a *makana*, gift, for you."

"Come to Kauai after you graduate." Pia rested a hand on my shoulder.

"Someday." Knowing that day would not be soon, I turned away.

When winter classes started, I took great care to avoid Sam, no small feat on such a tiny campus. Despite having different majors, we occasionally ran across one another. Once, I saw him holding hands with a girl, and did an about-face, walking all the way around Classic Hall to get to my meeting.

Until senior year, Education majors were separated, not only by discipline, but also by student age range: Early Childhood, Primary, Junior High, or Secondary. But in the last semester, all were required to gather twice a week to participate in mock classrooms. We took on student roles—class clown, anxious over-achiever, bully—challenging our "teachers" to deal with us on the spot. A faculty panel sat in the back, taking notes, and smiling often. The day Caro taught a practice class aimed at third graders, I became enchanted. First, she read a simple story about a lady wearing a green coat, boarding a train, then asked the class, "Who's the main character?"

"The lady, the lady!" we cried in unison.

"Good! And what did she ride?"

A bit of silence, then someone play-acting a shy pupil raised her hand in slow motion.

"Go on, speak up, Rosie, you know the answer." Caro's pretty smile and slight tilt of her head encouraged a response.

"A train."

"Yes!" Proud teacher eyes beamed praise toward the girl.

"Now, who can tell me the color of her coat?" We all waved. Some yelled, "Me, teacher, choose me!"

"Okay, class, quiet, please." Finger to her lips, Caro hushed the room.

"Red," Jim blurted out, with certainty.

Hands flew up once more, but, nodding, Caro kept her focus on Jim. "Close. Can you think of another color?"

"Yellow!" he shouted.

We waited to see how she would treat his answer.

"Absolutely right, Jimmy. Her coat was green."

All of us, including our professors, broke into laughter.

After class, Caro approached me. "It was bad, wasn't it? You can tell me the truth."

"Not bad." Still chuckling, I wound my scarf around my neck. "But really funny."

"We're not meant to threaten their self-esteem." Her soft, earnest voice made me look up.

"Yeah. That must be tricky with younger kids. Teenagers are tough." I pulled on my gloves. "Eager to argue."

"I don't know how anyone could ever teach high school." Shaking her head, she buttoned her jacket. "You must have a thick skin."

For some reason the comment bugged me, probably because it was true. Caro, not much bigger than many of my ninth grade girls, reminded me of Snow White, jet black hair, porcelain skin. Someone a prince could love forever. "They'd eat you alive." I grabbed my notebook.

"Don't be so sure." She picked up her book bag with one hand and tapped her chest with the other. "Deep down lives the heart of a panther."

We walked across the Quad, and she suggested hot cocoa in the Campus Center. Tucked into a vinyl booth, we began our friendship. Caro told me she'd transferred to Hanover last year from the University of Illinois. She liked our smaller college better, and hoped to find friends fast. "But campus life here is all about the Greeks. I'm way past that." She rolled her eyes.

"Oh." Waiting for her to notice my Theta sweatshirt, I scooped a marshmallow into my spoon.

"No offense."

"None taken. I'm really not much of a joiner, either, but Freshman Rush can be convincing."

"Glad I missed it, then." Caro grinned.

Morning coffee before class became our routine, and we bonded quickly. It hadn't been so long ago that I needed a friend. Finding Pia impossible to describe, I didn't share her with Caro, but I told her about Sam. Not everything, but enough.

"I'm still a virgin." She confided the information in a whisper. "But I don't mind. Mr. Right will show up and I've got years." Caro's way of talking made me laugh. Some words belonged in upper case, she called it Code. After listening to my stories, she christened Sam "Worthless Wretch," my prof, "Dr. Ducks," and Ian, "Smitten Briton."

"You don't mind that I'm not a virgin?"

"Vicarious Pleasure." She winked.

Senior assembly, requiring prospective grads to meet each Wednesday evening, began the second week of January. Alphabetical order put me next to the Danny McMahon, gorgeous campus playboy. "Hey there." His deep, sexy drawl pleased my ear.

Not trusting myself enough to speak, I smiled back. He stretched, making sure his arm grazed my breast.

"Hey, stop. That's enough." I grabbed his wrist before he could start groping.

"Really?" He winked. "Let's go get a drink."

"Maybe later," I whispered. "The speaker's just starting."

"Well, I'm out of here." He stood and headed for the men's room. "Meet me at Maggie's. Around eight." He didn't wait for my response.

When he saw me enter the bar, Danny sank back into the booth, motioning me to join him, as if inviting me to bed. His broad shoulders promised warmth from the cold, and I dove in close. His thumb went under my chin, raising my lips for a long kiss.

Both my hands tapped his chest. "You taste like a brewery."

"Easy fix." Grabbing the nearly empty pitcher, Danny got up, and put a hand on the table to steady himself. "Don't you go anywhere, now. Be right back."

"I'm not much of a beer drinker," I said.

"Oh, yeah, sweetheart?"

"Not such a sweetheart, either."

"You've got a mouth on you, all right." Looking amused, he put the pitcher down and shook his head. "What's your pleasure?"

The question, dripping with sex, excited me. "Cock." I paused. "Tail."

"Let's go, girl."

Outside on the street he asked me how I'd gotten there. "Borrowed a friend's car," I told him. Pia's, loaned to me until she returned.

"I hitched," he said, words sloppy. "Where you parked?"

Taking his hand, I led him around the block. As soon as we got in, I blasted the heat, and headed toward campus. The Point, a spit of land jutting into the Ohio River, was, by day, a scenic, romantic overlook, at night, the make-out hot spot. In winter, with engines running, the parking lot would look like a cloud and smell like exhaust fumes. Not appealing, but I couldn't think of another option.

During my college dating career, I'd been in a car on the Point only twice. Both times included heavy petting, but I never had sex in a car. Tonight, sheer animal attraction compelled me to the give in to the experience.

Even with the heat on, the car stayed cold. Danny began kneading my breasts through the cloth of my blouse. Uncomfortable and impatient, I guided his hand downward. While he explored, I unbuttoned, revealing nipples erect from the cold. He touched them, saying "Oh, baby, yes, baby," like a magic incantation. His rough kisses made me long for Sam's tender mouth.

Once I got my panties off and spread my legs, Danny's finger found me ready. He unbuckled his belt, unzipped his pants, and rolled a condom over his thick erection. Opening my legs wider, I slid down, scooting under the steering wheel. His penis, shorter than Sam's, made me think size did matter, and I resigned myself to no orgasm. So when Danny stopped grinding and began thrusting, the climax surprised me. He stayed inside while I caught my breath. Wriggling to free myself from his weight, I gulped air.

"Let me finish," he growled, and resumed jack-hammering. When he groaned, I held the back of his head, but did not kiss him.

"Lazy lady." Breath heavy, he climbed off. "Made me do all the work." Chuckling, he removed the condom and pulled a plastic bag, along with a twist tie from his pants pocket.

I struggled into my clothes. "You were prepared."

Missing my sarcasm, he burrowed next to me, attempting post-coital tenderness. I put the car in reverse. "Hey." He was still zipping his fly. "Slow down."

"Where can I drop you?" In spite of being the instigator, I regretted the sex.

"Uh-oh, doesn't sound good." Once dressed, he tried to fondle my breasts while I drove.

I swatted his hand away.

"Guess I don't get another date."

"You guess right."

"Let me out at the Phi Delt House." He handed me a card. "Call if you change your mind."

Irked by his arrogance, I crumpled the cardboard and made a face that told him we were done. Back at the dorm, I took a long, hot shower to wash the night away. Danny the Hunk, *Dunk*. I couldn't wait to tell Caro.

The next morning, before I had the chance, I saw her holding hands with Danny outside the bookstore. *Prick. He'd known we were friends.* His blonde stockiness made her look even tinier. Wondering how I was going to manage the rest of the school year without running into them, and Sam, I changed course. The list of people to avoid tripled, a moral dilemma added. Should I warn her? Caro relished talk about "doing it," but her inexperience made her easy prey. Danny would hurt her. Physically, because of her size. Emotionally, when she became a checkmark on his score card.

The next time we met for coffee, Caro seemed bubbly and energized. She was wearing make-up, blush across her pale cheeks and pink lipstick. Her hair tumbled from her trademark bun and fell over her tiny collarbone. "You like?" She wiggled her fingers in front of me to show off shiny, painted nails. "Danny says the red makes my hands look hot."

"Who's Danny?" Playing dumb might work.

"Only my new boyfriend, that's all!" She hopped up and down in the booth.

"Great, Caro." Trying to sound interested, even enthusiastic, I added, "Cool."

"Oh, he is." She sank back into the cushion, catching her breath. "Blonde. Blue. Tan. Phi Delt from Florida, Psych major. Built." She held up one red nail at a time to enumerate his qualities. I felt like one of her third grade students.

"Oh, yeah." I hesitated. "He sits next to me in Senior Assembly."

"Lucky." Caro leaned forward again. "Isn't he gorgeous?"

"You seem to think so."

"We've gone out twice this week." She lowered her voice. "I'm not going to graduate a virgin after all."

"Oh, Caro. Are you sure? Be sure. Is he Mr. Right?"

"Mr. Right's pretend." She laughed. "Girls who haven't done the deed use him as their excuse." She smoothed her hair.

"Be careful."

"Listen to you! You went for it with Sam."

"And look where that got me."

"What I really want to know is if you have any pills left."

"They take a while to work, Caro. And they make you fat."

"I don't care," she said.

"Sorry. I tossed them."

"Do you know anywhere I can get some?"

"Not really. Ask around."

"Oh I wouldn't ask anyone but you." She scooted her chair back and stood. "We grade school teachers have reputations to uphold."

Gathering my books, I didn't smile at her little joke. "I think you're making a mistake."

Caro put a hand on my shoulder. "Wish me luck?"

"He's no virgin." A pink flush was crawling up my neck. "Did you tell him you were?"

She waved her hand, dismissing the question. "You were lucky with Sam." Her voice softened. "Being firsts."

"Well." I cleared my throat. "Maybe you should consider waiting for someone worthy to share the experience."

"Worthy? The experience? God, Laura! When did you get so prissy? It's time for me to get laid and you know it."

"Point taken." I stood. "When do you see him again?"

"Tomorrow night. He's going to sneak me into the frat house. Says it beats a car."

Fearing she'd see the anger on my face, I turned my back and started walking.

"Help me pick out what to wear," she said when we got near her dorm.

"Now?"

"Please?"

Remembering how Pia had encouraged me to wear make-up and a sexy blouse, I nodded and followed her up the stairs. Caro held up several outfits, one by one, but each met with a head shake, until she pulled out a pale pink sweater dress, mini-length.

"Perfect for Valentine's." I touched the soft fabric. "Try it on." I reached for a pair of white boots. "With these."

While she changed, I sat on the edge of her bed and apologized to the photographs of her family.

"I look like a piece of strawberry candy." She came out of the bathroom and pulled at the hem with both hands. "Too short. I feel naked."

"Oh, come on, it's 1971. And you will be naked. Isn't that the whole idea?"

"Don't boys like to unzip, unbutton, and unhook?" She turned in front of the mirror.

"They also like to get right to the target." I stood. "You look adorable."

"Thanks, Laura." She came toward me for a hug.

On Mondays, I worked for Dr. Bucks in her home office. She'd published during the fall quarter, and her new deadline coincided with graduation. Usually I worked alone, typing from her longhand notes, checking annotations, re-reading for errors. That afternoon she bustled in around four. "Laura, the nice young gentleman from the bookstore, Ian, is here. He came by to deliver a British journal."

"That's kind of him." I glanced up, gave her a polite smile, and continued sorting papers.

"He's asking about you. Well, for you, really. Please join us for tea."

Since she was my employer, denying her request would have been pointless. I pushed my chair back. "May I have a few minutes to freshen up?"

"Certainly."

In the wash room I took inventory. The last time he'd seen me I'd been wearing a summer dress, flaunting my breasts, flirting my head off. Today my wool pants and loose sweater disguised every curve. No matter. Car sex with Danny soured me on men. I relaxed. No chance Ian would find me appealing.

Standing as I entered the room, Ian bowed his head. "Miss McKenna." My heart sped up at the sound of his voice.

"Please, sit." I could feel Dr. Bucks' delight at having the man in her house, a gentleman, no less, who spoke in a British accent and knew the Bard. "Mr. Harrington and I were discussing *English Journal's* latest article on Falstaff. Have you read it?"

"Not yet." Careful not to look at him, I allowed Ian to pour. Dr. Bucks could interpret body language as quickly as the blind could run their fingertips over Braille. Fearing she would sense my attraction, I kept my eyes on the carpet. "Please, continue your discussion."

As they examined the finer points of one of Shakespeare's most beloved characters, I sipped tea. When Dr. Bucks asked Ian a question he couldn't answer, he said, "I don't know," right away, without a trace of defensiveness. Every once in a while, he'd lick shortbread crumbs from the corners of his full mouth. Nearly an hour later, he stood, thanked Dr. Bucks, and extended his hand to me, brushing his knuckles against my fingertips. "Would you care to have dinner with me this evening?"

"Thank you, but I—"

"You're certainly caught up here, Laura." Dr. Bucks' eyes willed me to accept the invitation.

"Where's your coat?" Before I could follow, Ian returned from the office and slipped me, sleeve by sleeve, into my jacket, waved good-bye to Dr. Bucks and whisked me out the door.

"Are we in a hurry?"

"No." He opened the car door for me. "Afraid you might change your mind." He started the car. "And I didn't want to ask Dottie to join us."

"How come?"

His already ruddy cheeks flushed a brighter red. My question had been a tease, but he cleared his throat, stalling for an answer.

Amused that I could rile his oh-so-proper British manner, I let him off the hook. "Never mind. What I'd really like to know is how you ended up in Madison."

"Oh. Well. I was an English professor at Butler and didn't get tenure."

"Is that important?"

"For professors, yes." The car accelerated and he talked faster. "Without it, there are no guaranteed salary increases or promotions. Universities are businesses and must follow the law of supply and demand."

"Oh, I get it. Number of students and that sort of thing."

"Brilliant." He patted my thigh, and I leaned back, glowing at his compliment. He went on. "Majors and classes are offered based on enrollment. I should have been on the short list for Department Chair. Instead, the administration hired a bloke from New York. More selling power for their dodgy little college."

"That must have been disappointing."

"Quite." He turned in at the sign for Clifty State Park and slowed for the icy patches along the curving road. "Alas, English professors are in great supply and little demand, so I made the best of the situation. Madison Books was for sale, and I'm better off my own man." We pulled up in front of the lodge, a rustic building with lots of large windows.

Ambushed in work clothes, I kept my coat on in the restaurant. The place wasn't fancy, lots of high ceilings and thick, wooden beams, but I felt self conscious, especially because Ian looked dashing in a maroon V neck sweater. In summer, tourists could admire the powerful waterfalls, which generated much of the electricity for the Ohio River Valley, but the cold slowed the falls to a pace so modest they could barely be heard. Ian ordered for us. Two burgers, medium rare.

"Chips with that?" he asked. "Fries, that is."

"No, thanks. Let's have a drink, though."

"You go ahead. Get whatever you like. I'll pass."

Feeling awkward, I ordered a fancy cocktail.

"Rusty Nail, eh? Where did you hear of that?"

"From a friend." Drambuie was a favorite of Pia's. "Want a sip?"

"No, thanks, I don't drink."

"Oh, sorry." *Something to do with his not getting tenure?*

"Quite all right." Ian picked up his water glass. "Cheers!"

Eager to start conversation, I made a comment about the artwork. Ian looked bored. One of Pia's first lessons came to mind: men like to talk about themselves. "Tell me about your accent." Sure enough, Ian launched into an elaborate explanation of his heritage. "Upcountry Pict married Anglo Saxon, way back." He looked to my face for understanding, but my lack of knowledge about British geography made me unable to participate in the conversation. The warm power of the scotch made me uninterested and sleepy. When the meal came, we ate in silence and declined dessert.

Even though it was early, I asked him to take me back to the dorm. With the car heater blasting, conversation stopped until we parked in front of an apartment building on the edge of town.

"Want a real treat?" Ian put his hand on my knee.

Last summer his double meanings seemed clever, but now I found them childish. I shifted my legs. "Some other time?"

"No time like the present." Ignoring my answer, he got out of the car and came around to open my door. "Vintage posters. Gielgud's Hamlet, Olivier's Othello, quite a variety. You'll like them."

"Okay. But only for a few minutes." I followed him around the back of the building, upstairs, onto a wide balcony. In the glow of the porch light he looked old. "Do come in, pet."

"This isn't a good idea, after all." I turned toward the stairs.

"Oh, no you don't." Ian put strong hands on my shoulders. "You got away once." His King's English held an edge. "Shan't let that happen again."

"Listen, I'm tired." Hoping to end the uncomfortable scene, I forced a yawn. "Maybe another day."

"Stop being such a tease, Laura." He steered me into the apartment. Reaching for a decanter, he poured dark-gold liquid into two glasses. "Cheers." Ian took a deep swig before handing one to me. "Bottoms up, Luv."

"You said you didn't drink." I set my glass down, hard, on the kitchen counter.

"I don't." He took another swallow and set the decanter on a low coffee table. "In public." Emptying his glass, he reached for mine.

My eyes, checking for posters, moved across the walls of the living room.

"Relax." Ian perched on the arm of an overstuffed chair. "Take off your coat."

I shook my head.

"Have a seat." He patted the cushion and knocked back the second drink. "Come on, now, don't play the innocent little co-ed."

"You're drunk."

He pointed his index finger at me. "Last summer, you all but boffed me in the book shop."

"I may have led you on." I tossed my head and backed a few steps toward the door.

"May have?" His mouth made an O of mock surprise. "That's rich. Waving your knockers in my face, chatting about the heat. Pretty clear you wanted into my bed." Smoothing thick hair back from his forehead, he preened.

"Last summer I was confused."

"You were sleeping with that tall fellow."

"Do you know Sam?"

"I hoped you'd be ready for a man." Ian waited for a reaction, got none.

Forcing myself not to show fear, I stood still.

"I won't push." He tapped his fingers against his glass. "No, not me, the proper chap." The words carried a disturbing, sing-song quality. "I know you're experienced, trained by a pro."

"What are you talking about?"

"Before you started going to her little house in the woods, even before her oh-so-perfect husband died, Pia and I started shagging." He tumbled into the chair and grinned up at me. "Every Sunday, noon to two, we'd go into her bedroom. Behind a closed door, to be sure, but Hubby could hear our moaning."

"That was his idea ..., because he couldn't—"

Ian put up his hand. "Don't defend her. After he died, we broke off for a few months. Right around the time you came into her life, the strumpet threw me over for a rich boy."

"You..." In shock, I paused, "...don't know anything."

"Oh, yes, because I watched." His eyes widened. "Saw you two birds having your drinks, tarting up, wearing bras instead of blouses." Nodding, he poured another splash of whiskey.

"How?" I challenged.

"Thick summer leaves, a high river bank."

My mind raced, and the scotch from dinner burned its way up my throat, forcing me to take a few deep breaths. "You sick peeper," I started. "That's why you didn't get tenure."

I expected him to stop me, but my hand was on the door knob before he spoke. "No one had proof." As Ian followed me down the stairs. I tried not to run.

"I'll tell Dr. Bucks what I saw," he called. "Ruin you."

Turning to face him, I shrugged. "Go ahead. Explain how you were spying. After she talks to the English Department at Butler, no one here will buy your books." By this time, I was prancing sideways from one foot to another, a bully on the kindergarten playground. "Ruin you."

"Shall we call a truce, then?" Courtesy oozed back into his voice. "You're smashing."

"Two-faced pervert…," my rant fizzled. Whether he'd had sex with Pia didn't matter. I walked away, through the parking lot, toward the street.

"But nothing happened," he whined after me.

Plenty was happening inside me. On the long walk home in the winter dark, I thought about the things he'd watched: the makeover, our Hawaiian outfits, waiting for the guys. Pia, taking time and care, had grown me up. A quick visit to Caro's closet and my lack of honesty made me a bad friend. I hoped it wasn't too late. I'd call her first thing in the morning.

"Please tell me there's more to it than that," she began. Her back against the bed, Caro sat on the floor of her room.

"What happened?" I joined her on the floor.

"We hardly talked."

"Talking isn't required."

"Danny didn't look at me. Just shoved his thing…" The index finger of one hand moved back and forth through a fist of the other.

"You built yourself up, Caro." I touched her shoulder. "Sex isn't roses every time."

"I know." She took both my hands. "Please tell me there's more."

"Yes, you'll see." I gave her hands a squeeze. "Mr. Right, remember?"

"Not that we're keeping score, but we're even now." Her tone changed. "One and done?" She dropped my hands.

Puzzled, I gave a nervous laugh.

"God, Laura, did you think he wouldn't tell me? With every thrust he bragged how much you'd liked it."

My stomach churned. "Oh, God, Caro, I'm sorry."

"You should be."

"I didn't know." Even to me, the defense sounded pathetic.

"Sure. Maybe when you whored it up in the car, but afterwards—"

"I wanted to warn you." My voice cracked.

"Right."

"You don't believe me?"

She crossed her arms. "Get out."

"Wait a minute, I—"

She stood and grabbed her coat. "You won't leave, I will."

"Can't we talk?" I got up.

She opened the door. "No."

"But—"

"Leave. Me. Alone."

As she stormed down the hall, I followed close behind her. Caro turned, panther heart showing through her eyes, and slapped me across the face. The blow stung, and I stood still, catching my breath while Caro stomped ahead. The chimes for morning classes began, and several girls rushed into the hallway. I turned my face away while they filed by.

The next week proved long and miserable. I skipped Senior Assembly so I wouldn't have to see Danny, and sat in the back of Practicum, avoiding Caro. When Dr. Bucks asked about Ian, I gave a rehearsed speech. Yes, we had a delightful dinner. No, I didn't think I'd see him again. Thank you, no need to invite him for tea. Mulling over my various sins, I ate little and slept fitfully. I wrote Caro countless apology letters in my head. I prayed.

Caro found me at the Campus Center. "I knew you'd be here," she chirped. The third grade teacher was back. "I can't stay mad at you." Plopping down into the booth, she scooted close. She waited, making sure I would accept her hug. Both of us sniffled a little.

"Let's go after Danny," I started. All week I'd been plotting revenge.

"Okay, but—"

"How much do you want him hurt?"

"You sound like Mafia or something." She giggled. "What do you mean?"

"Should he be the victim of a humiliating, cruel practical joke?"

"Sounds good."

"Or should we get him kicked out of school?" I twirled my straw, making waves in my Coke. "Or both?"

"I think we should let the boy graduate."

"Okay. Let's start a rumor he's got VD. Picked it up last weekend from a whore in town."

Caro made a face. "Gross."

"Nobody will touch him the rest of the year."

Caro's nod encouraged me to continue.

"Whoever he makes moves on will treat him like a leper."

"Oooh, this'll be fun to watch." Her head bobbed. "Let's start this afternoon, at the first class break. A couple of his frat brothers are Ed majors. Give them an earful, too."

"Good idea. His roommate will move out. The rec room will empty at his approach." My voice carried a triumphant gloat. "Nobody will sit with him at meals."

Caro paused. "What if he retaliates? Says ugly stuff about us?"

"No doubt he already has."

"True." She looked down at the table for a moment before raising her eyes to mine. "But this would drag us into the gutter right along with him."

"Excuse me?" I leaned forward into her face. "Don't you want to take him down for what he did to you?"

"All I want is for things to go back to normal," Caro said.

"What's normal look like?"

"You and me, friends again."

"Done." Relieved, I took a deep breath. The week without her felt endless.

"Me, a Born-Again Virgin."

I chuckled. "Really?"

"Surely a girl who waits long enough can reclaim status." She sipped her soda, then looked up at me. "Even you."

Wondering if her comment was a dig, I smiled anyway. No chance I'd offend her again.

"After we leave this place, no one will be the wiser." Looking proud of herself, she sat back.

"Sounds good, but I have to sit next to Danny at assembly for six more weeks."

"He won't make a big fuss in a room full of people, especially if you focus on the speaker."

"Okay." I reached for her hand and squeezed. "Thanks."

On Wednesday, imagining Danny, I practiced faces in the mirror, but I couldn't manage to look livid and nonchalant at the same time. I decided keeping my back to him was the best option. On the way to assembly, I tried to ignore the knot in my stomach. Arriving early, I established my territory with props. By the time Danny slid into his seat my face was buried in a thick paperback. "Hey there," he started.

Pretending not to hear him, I cleared my throat, set the book down, and picked up a pen. The presenter approached the microphone. "Good evening, seniors." While close to two hundred voices wished him a good evening back, Danny took the opportunity to speak again. "Want another chance?"

Ignoring him, I shut my notebook and slipped everything into my book bag.

"Great," he whispered. Misinterpreting my actions, he started to stand.

I shook my head and pointed a finger in his face. "Sit, stay." I kept my voice low.

"Meet at Maggie's again?" He looked confused.

"Roll over," I said. "Play dead."

"Huh?"

When he didn't follow, my gut relaxed and my brain went into overdrive. Anything I might have said about taking advantage of Caro and me wouldn't have mattered. Danny would have pointed out, rightly so, that each of us consented to the act. Many college guys, girls, too, used sex for social standing, and perhaps no real harm came from their exploits. But Caro was right, soon we'd leave. In the real world, we could reinvent ourselves, and boys would have a chance to act like men. I had to laugh at the thought. Ian claimed to be a man, but, despite his refined exterior, turned out to be a slime-ball. Antony's tragic flaw, Cleopatra, and Lady Macbeth with her ambitious, blood covered hands did little to give me faith that women would turn out any better.

Most senior girls were engaged to be married, a few were going off to grad school, but I was desperate to leave the Midwest, equally desperate not to go alone. Caro and I applied for teaching jobs, hoping to land in the same town or county. One afternoon, carrying a thick folder of applications, Caro met me at our usual table in the Campus Center. "Mack," she began, her code for my last name, "I got a car."

"How?"

"My folks. For graduation."

"That's a generous gift." I felt a blip of envy.

"But it's a stick shift," Caro said. "I don't know how to drive it."

"Perfect. We can learn together."

When the weather was good, we practiced in the parking lot of a large store, Wal-Mart, being built off the new interstate. Construction debris that littered the expanse of asphalt, gave us an opportunity to shift often, inexpertly. One afternoon, after a session of what she called Meat Grinding, Caro parked, dug into her book bag, and pulled out a letter. "Dear Miss DeWitt, Blah, blah." She touched my shoulder. "The Poudre School District is pleased to offer you a position as a sixth grade teacher at Kruse Elementary." She bounced up and down in the seat.

"Younger kids would be better for me, but—"

"Caro, you got a job, a real job!" Even though my heart was sinking, I smiled.

She made her hand into a microphone started humming "So Far Away."

"Way out west. Lucky you."

"Come with me."

"Oh, Caro, there's no way."

"But why?" Her mouth turned downward, a childish pout.

"My parents have made it clear. After graduation, I'm on my own. My little job with Dr. Bucks gives me a thin cushion, but not enough to travel, pay for gas, set up an apartment in another town."

"My family will help both of us," Caro said.

I shook my head. "Thank you, that's really kind, but I couldn't—"

"I knew you'd say 'no.'"

"Sorry."

"Think about it, anyway. Promise."

"I will."

"Epic road trip."

"Huh?"

"Two girls head west in a car neither one of them can drive." Caro made her voice sound like a newscaster. "Strapping young men show up along the way to assist the damsels in distress."

"But they refuse all help," I continued in the same tone, "and learn to rely on themselves."

"Right on, Laura." She practically clapped her hands.

During spring break, most people left campus, but seniors were allowed to stay in the dorm. Even though Easter came in mid-April, egg hunts and picnics had to be moved indoors because of snow. But the following week, the sun coaxed bulbs to bloom and dogwoods to flower. Caro drove her car back to Illinois to visit her family, and I lacked a playmate, until Pia called. "Tutu's on the mend. I'm coming home."

"Fantastic."

"How about an early graduation present?"

"Sure."

"Let's make the trip to Angel Mounds."

"I'm ready." The thought of a whole week with Pia made me giddy. "Now that the weather's turned, we can camp."

"My tent's stuffed up high in the studio closet, and needs to be aired out. Check with my tenants first. They already know I'm arriving soon. Also, climb up and see if there's a cook stove on top of the tall art cupboard."

"Will do. This sounds like fun."

Pia looked out of place in the Louisville airport. After four months under Hawaiian sun, her honey colored skin deepened to a glowing amber, her dark hair held traces of gold. She wore a bright red sun dress, splashed with yellow flowers, a white sweater over her shoulders. Women in high heels clicked along the walkway to the baggage area, but Pia, in sandals, seemed to glide.

I felt oddly reserved. Pia had always been exotic, but now she seemed foreign. On the drive home, she told me a little about the beauty of Kauai, then leaned back in her seat and closed her eyes. "I'll be moving back to Berkeley," she said, without explaining why. "I'll keep renting out the house, but, after graduation, you can live in the studio as long as you want."

Moved by her offer, I paused. "Thank you. Maybe. I don't want to stay around here."

"What's wrong with here?"

"My entire life's been in the Ohio River Valley." I pulled into her driveway. "Both you and Caro will be far away."

Pia nodded and opened the car door. "I understand," She looked toward the house. "A change of scenery can make all the difference."

Another spring snow storm began as we drove to Angel Mounds. The fat flakes melted as they hit the windshield, and the flat fields out the window became frosty pillows. A subtle electricity charged the air as we entered the historic site. Due to the weather, tourists were few. The guard at the gate handed us a pamphlet and waved us through without charging admission. Inside, we strolled along wet paths that wound through what once was a village, and the man-made mountains seemed to exist only for us. "The state bought the property from the Angel family in 1938," I read.

"That would have been the chiefdom's main lodge." Pia gestured toward the conical land mass. "By the time Europeans arrived here, these guys were long gone. Same with the Hawaiian Islands." She took me by the elbow and kept talking as we walked the perimeter of the circle. "No one really knows exactly why, or when, or even who came and went."

"You do."

She laughed. "Because I've been here many times. When Charley was on the road with his rig, I'd walk over from the Draper farm, just over that ridge." Pia pointed to a space between the dwellings. "Only a few miles." She shivered. "The snow's enough to sour camping for me. Maybe we should ask them for shelter later on."

"I go where you go."

We spent the rest of the day wandering around the park. Late afternoon we snacked on some of our camping food in the car. At dusk we knocked on the front door of Pia's in-laws. Ben answered. "What a surprise." He sounded puzzled, not pleased.

"Hi, Ben." Even though he hadn't said "come in," we did. "You remember Laura?"

"Hello again," he said, offering his hand.

"We're on an adventure, exploring the mounds, were planning to camp and it's still snowing. Will you put us up for a night or two?" She said it fast, as if it would be easier for him to say yes if he really didn't have much time to think.

"Mama and Pop are already settled for the night."

"Please don't disturb them on our account," Pia said. "We can tiptoe through the hall to the back bedroom where Charley and I used to stay."

"Okay." Ben peered out the window. "Janet, Jim, and the kids are coming over for spring break, but not until Thursday. The room's all made up. No harm in letting you two use it."

He pulled back the curtain, and we all looked out. By then it was dark, cold enough for the snow to coat the landscape. The fact that Pia balked at camping surprised me. Most often she seemed so in tune with nature, her temperament adapting easily to each season. The night sky revealed the stars, extra bright and crisp, little bonfires across a vast black sea. "Beautiful," I said.

"We don't have much." Before Ben or I could help, Pia went to the car and came back with our two small duffels and a briefcase. We stayed in the kitchen for a while and made small talk over cups of hot tea. Ben told a long story about how he, as a boy, camped in snow. Pia fidgeted, not really listening, so I tried to nod at the appropriate moments.

My thoughts wandered to Charley. I hoped he'd been more entertaining than his brother. Pia seemed anxious to retire. It wasn't late enough to be genuinely sleepy, but I forced a yawn, and Ben got the message. He tiptoed down the hall, our bags in hand, and whispered, "Goodnight."

Pia closed the door to the farmhouse bedroom, then leaned back against it and exhaled.

"What's that about?" I asked.

Motioning me to sit next to her on the bed, Pia opened the briefcase. "These deeds are for our land and house near Madison." She removed a folder, shuffled through several pieces of paper, and showed them to me one by one. "You already know that Charley's parents co-signed the loan we took to build the house." She held up another document. "We put up the land as collateral. The mortgage got paid regularly until right before the end, when Charley defaulted in order to put funds aside for me." Returning all papers but one to the folder, she asked if I was following so far. When I nodded, she went on. "See this?" She waved the page in front of my face. "Funny how one piece of paper can cause so much trouble."

The page didn't look official. Unlike the other documents, white certificates with formal language and notarized signatures, this sheet of paper had a slightly blue-grey tinge, words handwritten, letters wobbled. "Charley," I guessed.

"Yes. No one but me has ever seen this. Charley deeded the house and land back to his folks."

"I don't understand."

"He was crazy with pain at the time. In my heart, I know he wasn't thinking clearly, that he wanted to reunite with them at the end, give them something of value." Her voice broke, and she hesitated.

"Nobody's seen it. You're sure?"

She studied the page. "Absolutely."

"Then why not destroy it?"

"I promised him."

"Of course. You had to." I paused. "Then, but now—"

"He told his sister."

"When?"

"The day before he died. Janet showed up, marched right in and practically elbowed me out of the way. 'Take a break,' she told me. I'd been up with him the better part of the night. Couldn't have been gone more than half an hour. A shower, a bite of food. A few weeks later, when the will was read, Janet kept quiet."

"Until the day last summer when they all came to visit."

Pia nodded. "Tutu helped me delay the inevitable, but now I have to honor his last wishes."

Her little house had been my home, too. The fact it would no longer be hers made me feel lost. "What about the studio?" I pressed my hand, palm open, against my heart.

"Never a part of the deal. We didn't apply for permits and relied on Charley's trucker buddies for the construction. Charley's will left the studio to me, regardless who owns the land."

I exhaled. "Wonderful."

"On top of that, I have a guardian angel."

"Who?"

"Remember Kevin Parker?"

"Your gorgeous young lover? How could I forget?"

"He lives in Boston now. Last month he turned twenty-three and inherited a fortune." Pia slipped the handwritten page back into the folder. "He says I supported him at a time in his life when he felt confused, that I helped him make important decisions. Good ones."

"I can totally relate."

"We've kept in touch." She placed the folder into the briefcase. "Last year he bought several pieces of my art."

"Good that he appreciates your work." I wished I had something to offer Pia. "Sounds like he's turned out to be much more than just a pretty face."

"Pretty, yes. Inside and out." She smiled and closed the briefcase with a click. "He's made the Drapers an offer for the house and land."

"Are they going for it?"

"Absolutely. They'd be crazy not to." She turned back the covers on the bed. "As beneficiary of the Parker-Draper Trust, I can stay, or be there, whenever I want, for the rest of my life."

"Oh, so that's why we're here?"

"Sort of. Kevin offered to handle the transaction, and Ben didn't expect me to come in person. Makes him uncomfortable."

"Then why did you?"

"Tutu told me to wipe the slate clean. At first I resisted, thinking that staying connected to them the rest of my life would honor Charley, but now I understand." Pia pulled a nightgown from her duffel bag. "Get your PJs on. Take the big bed."

Tucked under the blankets on the pull-out sleeper, I closed my eyes. Pia sang a soft melody. Long words, full of vowels, lulled me into sleep.

The next morning, I made pancakes for Mr. and Mrs. Draper in the rustic kitchen while Pia and Ben went to the bank to finalize the wire transfer. Pia, glowing when they returned, asked Ben to join us in the park for the rest of the day. Claiming chores, he refused.

"They're all so weird and quiet," I said when we were in the car.

"Because I remind them of Charley."

"Do they remind you?"

"The place does. Not the people. He may have come from them, but he wasn't one of them."

"That's the way I am with my folks."

She nodded. "Me, too."

Better weather brought spring breakers. Kids arrived with grandparents. Teens, oblivious to anyone, other than themselves, gathered in groups large enough to prevent a clear view of some of the dwellings. We sought sanctuary inside, where a park ranger was lecturing a group of scouts. Pia and I sat on a bench in one of the alcoves of the museum and listened.

"Everyone thinks a kingdom has one king, a chiefdom, one chief, but, two hundred years before this Native American settlement, Polynesians set a precedent for elaborate interconnectedness."

This really got our attention.

"On Hawaii, Maui, Kauai, and Oahu, royalty worked together."

"Not always." Leaning forward, Pia whispered. "When *ali'i* first came to the Islands, they misunderstood the kind of power, *mana*, respected by the native people. The outsiders waged war, not only against the Islanders, but each other."

We turned our focus back to the ranger. "The land a man settled on became his residence, but not his property."

"Yes." Pia nodded. "The royalty eventually learned to respect the community system of the original inhabitants."

"Historians and archeologists often assess a culture based on size: bigger means better, more powerful, dominant," the ranger continued. He stood in front of a map with shaded areas and a key too small to read from where we were sitting.

"Here," he tapped an area with a wooden pointer, "the Mississippian culture built a town on a large, terraced mound. For nearly three hundred years, the inhabitants traded with other peoples along the Ohio and Mississippi Rivers."

Pia and I listened raptly, but the scouts became restless, shuffling and whispering. The ranger raised his voice to continue. "One of the most fascinating ceremonial characteristics is the burial mounds." His loud announcement had the desired effect.

"Did you find dead bodies?" one kid asked.

"Not me, personally, but a team dig last summer brought out remains from along the plaza platform." Searching the map, the ranger paused. "Bones, actually, from Temple Mound."

The scouts drew closer. A chorus of whispers about skeletons and ghosts followed. One boy said, "That's gross. Can we see?"

"Not yet. We're still figuring out who they might have been."

Disappointment caused them to become distracted once again. Their leader mentioned lunch, and we sat alone.

"Charley's buried here." Pia was still whispering. "Not in the mounds, of course, but in a graveyard near their church."

"How come?" The news surprised me. "I thought you'd want him close."

"No matter how much I tried to explain the old ways...," Pia's breath caught before she went on, "...the Drapers couldn't understand." She paused. "Bones, *iwi,* are sacred, and contain the spirit of the loved one. Traditional natives respected, even guarded the skeletons."

"But can't you bring flowers and gifts to the cemetery?"

She laughed. "Sure. And kneel before a gray slab that has his name carved on it, as if that's all he was. The family, *ohana*, maintained burial sites in old Hawaii as shrines. The dead would continue to bless the living."

"Does Hawaii have graveyards?"

"Of course, many, but most burial sites were desecrated years ago."

"Do you ever visit Charley at the church?"

"Rarely. It holds little meaning for me. But today I'm going one last time."

"To say goodbye?"

"To take him with me. Tutu taught me how." She stood and we walked outside.

Later, I waited in the car while she walked through the cemetery, an uncrowded and pleasant place. The graveyard sat alongside a white brick church. A simple wrought iron fence enclosed about twenty tombstones. Bouquets of fresh flowers at the base of several stones looked especially bright against winter's brown grass. She didn't kneel, sing, talk, or hesitate at his tomb stone. She looked down at the ground, up at the sky, brought her hands toward her heart in a scooping motion. I imagined Charley's essence flowing into her.

We didn't talk on the way back to the farm. It wasn't a time for questions, although I had a few. And we didn't stay. Pia spoke to both Mr. and Mrs. Draper and hugged them close.

She went out to one of the barns in search of Ben, and I didn't witness their parting.

Pia asked me to drive, directing me to a campground about a half hour away. The natural springs and waterfalls were cold, but we put our feet in and splashed each other so many times we felt thoroughly baptized.

When Pia left for California, she handed me the key to the studio. We were standing at the top of her driveway, awaiting her cab to the airport. Tears were building behind my sunglasses, and I couldn't speak, but she had the perfect words. "The unknown can be wonderful." She touched my shoulder. "I can't wait to see what you'll do next."

"Me, either." I tried to sound excited.

"We've been apart many times. I went all the way across the ocean for nearly half a year, remember?" Reaching over, she lifted my sunglasses to the top of my head. "Everything's always worked out fine." She smiled.

"Because I'm always here when you come back."

"And, if you're not here, if, by chance, you've found a teaching job and moved away, I'll forget about you. Is that it?"

"I don't know."

"Neither do I, but it's highly doubtful." She smiled again. "And I hope you're not here the next time," she looked at her watch, "so we can find out." Pia pulled me into her arms. "Go on, now," she whispered into my hair. A sob rose to my throat, and I made a croaking sound that caused us to break apart and laugh. A car, the cab, slowed, coasting onto the shoulder. Pia blew kisses in my direction, and, feeling empty already, I turned and walked down the driveway.

Classes for the year were almost finished, and most afternoons, Caro and I met for coffee. Often we'd sit at a table on the patio under the shade of large-leafed tulip trees. At the start of May, all I could think about was Sam's last birthday. I confided in Caro, telling her the story about how Sam's dad kicked me out.

"This is my anniversary of shame." My mind replayed the Judge's harsh words. "Every time I think about it, I want to crawl under a rock."

"So?" Caro said, without sympathy in her tone. "What does one grouchy old man matter?" She waved her hand, dismissing the matter. "You're way too young to have a pity party."

"But—"

"Remember how fast we put Danny behind us?" She waved again.

"Different." Leaning back, I crossed my legs. "I got to talk back to Danny."

"Big woo-hoo." Caro huffed. "If you're going to be defensive, why bother telling me? I thought perhaps you wanted a fresh perspective." She waited for my slight nod to continue. "You're angry with yourself." Looking pleased at her announcement, she slapped a hand onto the table.

"Oh come on, Caro, I'm not a little kid in your classroom. I don't need a row of smiley faces, or an angry mouth to help me understand my 'feelings.'" Baring my teeth, I said, "Grrrr."

She laughed. "All righty, then, Miss Know-It-All, be mad at Sam, if that helps."

"Nothing helps."

"Let's go to Decatur for the weekend," Caro suggested. "Get things off your mind, show you my hometown."

We took off in Caro's car, grinding the gears, confusing clutch with brake, as we practiced shifting on long stretches of Illinois flatland. Normally the trip took four hours. We made it in six. Caro's family lived in a roomy two story surrounded by an open field. In spring, the alfalfa bloomed light purple, making the landscape rural. "You live on a farm?" I asked.

"No. Right now it looks like a meadow," Caro said as we drove up. "Most of the year it looks weedy." We got out of the car and walked around the side of the house. "Used to be a crop. Most everything in Illinois used to be a crop."

Caro's mom met us before we reached the door. She gave her daughter a hug, then turned and gave me one. "Laura."

"Hello," I said into the top of her head.

Almost as petite as Caro, Nancy Benson looked close in age to my mother, but her personality seemed opposite. "Get your stuff, girls, and come on in. We're having a little get-together in your honor."

Caro beamed and gently elbowed me. "See. Told ya. Let the good times roll. Just throw your stuff on the bed. We don't need to dress up," Caro said after we brought our duffels in. "Meet me downstairs."

Her childhood room contained twin beds and a tall bureau. Ignoring her instructions, I reached into my bag for a fresh blouse. Then I opened the closet to hang the wrinkles out of the rest of my clothes. There I found fashion evidence of

Caro's younger days, a pretty ballerina dress, a cowgirl Halloween costume, a prom gown. Each carefully covered in plastic, saved, treasured, honoring special times in her life.

Where were my childhood clothes? I'd not taken ballet, but did ice skate in *The Nutcracker* one winter. What about the Indian princess get-up, the pink taffeta tea dress, my senior year formal? Mom must have saved them somewhere. Shock treatments erased memories, but which ones?

"Hey, Laura, come on!" Caro's call from the bottom of the stairs interrupted my reverie.

"On my way."

Reaching the kitchen, I gave a small yelp of surprise. Mrs. Benson had prepared platters of colorful appetizers: red and gold sweet peppers, stuffed with soft herb cheese, black and green olives, tiny rye toasts to dip into sour cream. *A far cry from celery sticks filled with peanut butter, Ritz crackers, cheese from a squirt-can.*

"Isn't this great? Here." Caro handed me a tray to carry out onto the screened back porch. "Mom's in heaven when a crowd's coming."

"My folks don't entertain often," I said.

"She's definitely ahead of the pack, even bakes cakes from scratch." Caro sounded proud.

The guests included a few neighbors, along with lawyers from Mr. Benson's small-town practice, and a couple of Caro's friends from high school. Everybody, especially her parents, made a big fuss over her. "To our daughter." Mr. Benson raised a glass of sparkling wine. Caro's father reminded me of Gregory Peck as Atticus Finch, handsome and wise.

"Graduating next month," he went on. Light clapping. "Employed!" More applause.

Caro's mother waited for quiet. "Did everyone receive invitations to the ceremony? Make sure to RSVP. We're hosting a luncheon afterwards at Hill House."

"Join us," Caro whispered.

"Can't. We've got reservations, too."

"Your people can sit with my people."

"Maybe." I took a bite of sliced cucumber and tried to think of an excuse. "I don't think it's a good idea."

"How come?"

"My folks don't socialize much."

"Mom will work something out."

"That's kind, but please don't," I said, enough seriousness in my voice to make Caro pause. I reached for another glass of wine and went to mingle with the other guests.

Sunday morning, instead of going to church, we sorted through Caro's wardrobe. "You'll need professional clothes," her mother said. "Let's plan a shopping trip to St. Louis in late June. Can you come along, Laura?" I thanked her and nodded, knowing I wouldn't go. My time needed to be spent finding a job.

Caro squeezed my arm. "We'll stay at the Chase."

"Invite your mom," Mrs. Benson said. "I'd love to meet her."

"Okay." Inside I cringed. The Bensons seemed to have no dark secrets, and I wondered how much longer I could keep my family from meeting them. Covering for Dad became second nature, but Mom would be no match for the chatty, intelligent Nancy Benson.

The rest of the day Caro drove me through town. She pointed out her elementary school, her dad's office, her mother's woman's club. "My little life," she said. "Now you see why I couldn't wait to get out."

"I think it's wonderful."

"You're right." She pulled the car to the curb. "Three years at UI filled me with anxiety. Too much competition. Academically and socially."

"Good thing you transferred."

"I know. What has me worried, though, is that Hanover's nothing like the real world." Caro tapped her fingers on the steering wheel. "Maybe I should stick around the Midwest after all." She glanced sideways toward me.

"Oh, no, Caro Benson, you're going. No pity party for me, no shying away from life for you."

She laughed. "Fair enough."

After dinner Mr. Benson touched my shoulder. "Laura, do you have a minute to help me with something in the study?"

Here it comes. I knew this family was too good to be true. Despite my misgivings, I followed him to his home office, and was relieved when he didn't close the door. Motioning me to a chair, he sat behind his desk. "An investment in your future." Mr. Benson cleared his throat and handed me an envelope. Reluctantly, I peeled back the flap, and unfolded a check for five hundred dollars. "Caro knows nothing," he said. "In fact, she would be outraged."

I didn't believe him. She'd gone behind my back. While I sat there, searching for words, he went on. "She would accuse us of meddling, and, rightly so." He leaned forward and kept his voice low. "We don't want Caro going so far away by herself. Not that we don't have confidence in her…"

Placing the check on his desk, I shook my head. "Mr. Benson, I can't promise to—"

"We don't expect you to." He removed his glasses and took his time cleaning the lenses before settling them back onto his face. "We're, um, hedging our bets, so to speak. If the time comes for Caro to move, and you haven't found a job … employment, I mean, in your field, consider going with her." He scooted the check toward me. "If you do land a teaching position elsewhere, the money's yours to keep, regardless. A gift is a gift."

Touched by his concern and sincerity, I paused to reconsider. The generous amount would buy me two or three months, along with the chance to uproot, the opportunity I'd been longing for. "How do I explain my newly found resources?" I picked up the check. "Caro's like you. A lawyer. Wants to know everything."

"Tell her you received a graduation present from a long lost relative."

Without meaning to, I laughed. "Sorry. That might sound like a plausible explanation, but I can't get away with such a whopper. Caro knows me too well."

"Okay, hmm." He tapped the desk with a pen. A few moments later he said, "Caro's told me you work for one of your professors."

I nodded.

"Perhaps he—"

"She," I corrected him.

"Does Caro know her?"

"No, sir. Dr. Bucks is head of the English Department."

"Okay. That's it, then. Dr. Bucks gave you a bonus. You don't have to say how much."

My conscience struggled for only a moment. Folding the check, I stood and slipped it into my pocket. "My parents will believe that story as well."

"All the better." Mr. Benson came around to the front of the desk. Co-conspirators, we shook hands.

During the last two weeks of school, graduating seniors, usually separated by cliques, embraced one another. Students, who, for the last four years, barely acknowledged my existence, now spoke to me as if we'd been close. There was an implicit understanding that this was our last chance to act like idiots.

Late afternoons, the nearly-graduated gathered behind different frat houses for spontaneous parties. Caro and I attended two or three. We'd sip beer and listen to the music blasting from speakers propped up in windows. Sometimes musical battles ensued. Rock and roll, versus folk, or heavy metal. Once in a while, someone would turn off the sound, and we'd sing a sloppy version of the *Alma Mater.*

Campus cops, acting as though they, too, had been our best friends, ignored the ruckus. Dance contests, complete with making out and groping, made for additional fun. Public displays of affection were encouraged. Some of the more attractive senior guys, engaged or pinned to underclassmen, taking their chances on being forgiven by their partners, came on to all the senior girls. When the gatherings ended right after sunset, we rejoined our usual groups.

Rehearsals for the ceremony involved stepping up onto a makeshift stage and filing into rows of metal folding chairs. Seniors who had achieved academic excellence sat in a special section, exceptional athletes in another. The rest of us lined up alphabetically. Thankful that Danny majored in football, I chatted with the girls on each side and craned my neck forward to spot Caro up in the B section. All week she'd joked about how she would graduate before me. "Not true," I said. "At the end, we all stand and move our tassels at the exact same time."

"Yeah, but I get my diploma at least an hour ahead of you."

"You get a fake leather folder. After the ceremony, you swap cap and gown for the magic certificate." I rolled my eyes. "Haven't you been listening?"

"Who put a bug up your butt?" she asked. "Are you mad at me?"

"Not," I said. "Just can't wait to get out of here. Too many rules."

"The whole world has rules," Caro said. "Even Colorado."

"You sound like your dad."

"That's a good thing, right?"

The comment made me wonder if Caro suspected her parents were behind my good fortune.

True to my word, I had continued to apply for teaching jobs. Several school districts urged me to make contact again in January when the new semester started. But nothing held real promise, and, the week before graduation, I told Caro I'd go with her. We had just picked up our caps and gowns and were standing outside the bookstore. Expecting shouts of joy and happy tears, I'd been surprised at her response. At the news, she stood still for a moment. "Only if you're sure."

"Of course, I'm sure, why wouldn't I be?"

"You've still got so much going on here."

"I do?"

"Dr. Bucks would let you stay on. Not only would it be a feather in her cap to have her pet English major researching her articles, but she'd help you get a paper published. Once that happened, your career would be cake. Schools would court you. Maybe even junior colleges."

"You have a wild imagination, my friend. You flatter me."

"I know you. You're brilliant. Besides, what about Pia?"

"She's moved to Berkeley." Tears came to my eyes at the thought, and I looked away. "Didn't I tell you?"

"You'll want to be here when she comes back to visit."

"I can't base my whole life on her schedule."

"True," Caro said. "And, as much as I want you to come...," she draped her gown over one arm and used the other to hug me, "...you can't move to Colorado for me, either."

A knot inside me began to unravel. "You're the brilliant one."

She grinned. "Both of us are. We're graduating, remember?" She put on her cap, sideways.

"Look out, world!"

Commencement. Several hundred spectators sat in neat rows of chairs on the grassy area of The Point. Seniors marched onto the portable stage. In June, the river ran clear, and the white basswood trees along the banks were fully green. Mosquitoes and black flies had a standing invitation. The Class of 1971 looked small. Several former students were presently fighting a war. Their day would be spent with enemies that could do far more damage than biting insects.

Like other graduates that June, we were wearing caps and gowns in school colors, scarlet and gold. Had she been there, Pia would have laughed at what passed for scarlet. Our robes were a purplish, muddy maroon, the cheap material worn thin, shiny from repeated annual use. The gold, dingy, did not shine.

All college students fantasize about Commencement. "Pomp and Circumstance" is supposed to evoke pride and satisfaction. Four years spent in study, disciplines learned. For me, the ritual meant sitting in the hot sun, swatting bugs with my rolled up program, waiting for my name to be called. Mom, Dad, Meg, and her boyfriend, Robert attended. They piped a weak "Hooray" when the college president shook my hand. Earlier that day they were introduced to Dr. Bucks, English Department and Dr. Maricle, Secondary Education. My family had never met Pia, my Life Teacher, who held no degree.

Afterwards, graduates traded the awful caps and gowns for real diplomas, no longer sheepskin, but their calligraphy made them elegant. Mom took mine for safekeeping. "We're so happy, Laura." She held the parchment with both hands. "A black frame, with a thin gold line, perhaps? We'll hang it in the family room."

"Thanks, Mom," I said, thinking the display of my diploma was to enhance their social status, and immediately chiding myself for the thought. My mom hadn't finished college; she was simply proud that I had.

"We have reservations at Hill House," Meg announced. "Robert drove us up." Code between sisters: Dad won't be driving home drunk.

"Great." Looking over my shoulder, I spotted Sam leaning against a pillar at Classic Hall. "Give me a minute. I'll meet you at the car."

He wasn't exactly hiding, but trying to make himself smaller, an impossible feat. The endearing gesture, so typical, so Sam, gave me the courage to approach him. I stepped onto the porch where he stood. "Hey, Laura. Hi. " Opening his arms, he came toward me for a hug.

Wondering if physical contact might reawaken my desire for him, I avoided the embrace. Throwing my hands in the air, I said, "Hooray, we're done!" I tried to sound happy. "Are your folks here?"

He nodded.

"Congratulations," we both said at the same time.

I wanted to tell him that, although he'd broken my heart, he'd been my first love, and I'd always remember him. Instead, I said, "Good luck."

"Thanks." He looked at his shoes.

"What are you doing next?" I asked.

"Going up to Cincy to celebrate with cousins."

"That's nice." Staring at the space over his shoulder, I forced a smile. "I meant like a job, or something."

"Oh." He shifted his gaze to the top of my head. "Yeah." Sam shrugged. "Nothing solid yet."

"Me either."

"That's too bad."

"My family's waiting. Yours must be, too." I didn't want his sympathy and the conversation wasn't going anywhere. Turning, I waved goodbye over my shoulder. On the way to the parking lot, my internal soundtrack swelled with dramatic music. *He'll run after you, take you in his arms, apologize for everything, and propose marriage. Don't walk so fast, give him a chance to catch up.* I looked back and saw Sam heading in the opposite direction.

Recovering from my fantasy, I hobbled across the asphalt baking in the June sun. My feet, in strappy high heeled sandals, ached. Sweat drenched the armpits of my pretty dress. Robert honked, and I jumped. Mom rolled down the window. "Our reservations are for noon, Laura."

"Don't worry, it's just across the bridge." I got into the back seat. Going to Hill House was the last thing I wanted. Sam and I went there on our first date, the irony worthy of Shakespeare. My big day, my triumph, felt like personal defeat.

As soon as we entered the restaurant, Caro waved me over to a large banquet table. She stood, and we hugged. "Come on." She pointed to some empty place settings. "We have room."

"Looks like you brought the village." I stalled, figuring out how to decline gracefully.

"Laura, congratulations!" Caro's mom pulled me into a hug. "Please join us."

"Thank you." I looked over my shoulder. My family was being seated at a small table in the back corner. "Too late." Taking Caro by the hand, I led her toward our table. "Come meet everybody."

Later, Dad would need to be managed carefully. He'd be silent and slow until his first drink, happy with his second, jovial after his third. After that, he'd become belligerent and pick a fight with one of the waiters, or one of us. Mom would repeat the same questions: "Where did you get that dress, Laura? Did you color your hair again, Meg? Who's driving?"

But now Mom did her wonderful Southern thing. "I'm happy to meet you, dear." She cupped Caro's hands in both of hers. "Laura speaks so highly of you." Dad stood and gave Caro a big hug and a kiss on the cheek. Meg and Robert asked about Colorado, but I whisked her away before she could answer. "I haven't told them yet."

"You've decided." She took a deep breath. "I haven't told my folks, either. In case you weren't coming. They'll be glad. They pretend they're okay with me moving far away, but they're not very good pretenders."

"Well, don't say anything today, in case the parental paths cross." Leaving Caro with her tribe, I returned to my own. My people behaved better than I expected. Dad raised his highball glass toward me. "To my brilliant daughter." I basked in his praise. Mom said that my professors seemed impressed by my accomplishments. Mr. and Mrs. Benson came by to introduce themselves. Mom and Dad kept their act together, and I relaxed. After the meal, I asked to be taken back to the dorm. "Are you all packed up, honey?" Mom asked.

"Not quite. My stuff won't fit in the trunk. A friend will drive me down next week."

When we said goodbye, she looked disappointed, and I kissed her cheek. Dad was already snoozing in the back seat.

After changing into shorts and a tank top, I packed a small overnight bag, and walked down Devil's Backbone to Kate Hall. Most of the way, the summer shade shielded me from the heat, but, as I unlocked the studio, my heart hammered into my dry mouth. First priority, ice water, next, electric fan. Collapsing onto the bed, I stared at the murals, imagining the sound of the ocean, the sway of palms, knowing no one could find me.

As sunset drained the heat of day, gentle shadows fell, and I strolled toward the river, where a light breeze had chased away the bugs.

The water sings a twilight lullaby, and soothed, I listen, looking upward. My bundle has shifted, settling onto a low branch. I'm able to reach it with relative ease. As the cloth unwinds, the contents surprise me: a page from *Shakespeare's Sonnets*, a tiny, white card with a red *sold* dot, from the chickadee painting in Berkeley, beads from the art cupboard, a firecracker.

Sacred objects.

Our stories, like fairy tales, can be retold. Little girls wear navy blue because their aunt knows black frightens them. Let them sleep all afternoon and wake up good, loved by their father and his new wife, embraced by the beauty of their mother's poetry.

Enchantments can be broken. The angry father slumbers on the couch, a mother relinquishes her power. A young woman sets out from home and finds gods everywhere. Kneel, dive into water, and sing hymns. Act out the Bible, or chant, the world is church.

All of myself I gather. Here, now, my own belonging lives inside of me. As I walk out onto the sandy river bank, the trees become still, the calls of night birds ruffle the silence. Bending at the waist, graceful at last, I release my bundle into the water.

⋘ ⋙

Thanks to the La Playa Writers' Workshop for your
patience, encouragement, and enthusiasm.

Special thanks to Susie Parker and Ann Parker
for sharing their knowledge about and love of Hawaii.

Eternal thanks to Dave for your love.